A KNIFE AGAINST A GUN

And there he was, Bob Wells, bigger than life. "Tut, tut, Marshal, you don't want to go reaching for that gun," he said with a sly grin. "You just drop that rifle and six-gun and get down off of that horse nice and easy now and make your way on down here."

I did as he said, dropping my weapons and slowly climbing down from Chance's mustang, letting the reins drop to the ground. My mind was already trying to figure out a way to get out of this scrape, but for the life of me I couldn't figure one out. The only thing that did come to mind was the fact that I still had that tinker knife draped down the back of my neck. But as long as this Wells character had a gun trained on me, why, I'd likely die before I could put the blade in his sorry gullet . . .

Books by Jim Miller

Stagecoach to Fort Dodge
The 600 Mile Stretch
Rangers Reunited
Too Many Drifters
Hell with the Hide Off
The Long Rope
Rangers' Revenge

Published by POCKET BOOKS

7

THE EX-RANGERS

STAGECOACH TO FORT DODGE

JIM MILLER

POCKET BOOKS

New York   London   Toronto   Sydney   Tokyo   Singapore

An *Original* Publication of POCKET BOOKS

POCKET BOOKS, a division of Simon & Schuster Inc.
1230 Avenue of the Americas, New York, NY 10020

ISBN: 0-671-74825-4

First Pocket Books printing July 1992

10 9 8 7 6 5 4 3 2 1

Cover art by Garin Baker

Printed in the U.S.A.

For Ralph Allen, a real fighter,
especially when the chips are down.

STAGECOACH
TO
FORT DODGE

CHAPTER

★ 1 ★

Something about Monday mornings has always reminded me of the newness in life. I reckon it's mostly just people getting over the laziness of a Sunday, the one day of the week when as a rule a man could sit back and rest a while. The stores and shops are usually a mite slower opening up on Mondays, so the feeling must be about the same for near everyone in town. At least that's what I've always thought.

Of course, back in my youth, when I was a mountain man and after that a Texas Ranger, why, you could hardly tell one day from the next, nor did you care much. There always seemed to be too much to do back then to notice much more than Old Sol rising in the east and setting at nightfall. But those days were long gone, days that were mostly for storytelling about

1

over a sip of the hard stuff, if you get my drift. For more than a decade now I'd been used to city living, which is a whole different thing from roaming the plains in a pair of buckskins. Yes, sir.

According to my pocket watch it was going on nine o'clock as I finished making my first rounds of the city streets of Twin Rifles. I'd just come from Margaret Ferris's boarding house, where I did my sleeping and eating in those days, and a hearty breakfast of ham and eggs. Making that first walk through the streets had become a daily ritual, and it was then I mulled over the thoughts of Mondays and how slow they were.

"Morning, Marshal," Pardee Taylor said, nearly surprising me as he caught me walking in the opposite direction.

"Oh, morning, son," I said. I'd had my eye on the bank, calmly waiting for it to open up any minute now. "Where you headed?"

"Over to Kelly's Hardware." Pardee stopped suddenly, as though remembering something he'd forgotten and knew it was too late. A frown crossed his face as he dug in his pocket and came up with nothing. "Damn. I'm gonna have to take some money out of the bank, I reckon."

I could remember a time when I hardly ever saw Pardee Taylor standing straight up and tall. Usually he'd had an empty bottle attached to one of his fists and been looking for someone to bully into buying him another bottle. He'd succeeded, too, for a while, until he ran into Emmett, an ex–cavalry sergeant who'd just ridden into town and who wound up helping my boys break a whole mess of mustangs after a while. Emmett had beat the living hell out of Pardee, but it was a woman who did Taylor in. She chewed him up one side and down the other and never once used a cussword. As I recalled, it was the humblest I'd ever seen Pardee Taylor. That it was. It took almost a week for him to dry out, but he'd been doing his best ever since to stay sober and act like he belonged to the citizenry of Twin Rifles. He'd even offered to help me out a couple of times, but I'd never had anything I could oblige him with.

"Looks like you're just in time, Pardee," I said, watching the doors to the bank open.

We weren't that far from the jail and the office I kept, so I wasn't surprised to see Joshua step out onto the boardwalk and stretch and yawn. Joshua was my deputy. He spent most of his nights sitting up in an empty jail, me relieving him at nine, when the bank opened. Then he'd get a few hours of sleep and report back for duty about midafternoon. He'd been with me about four years now, I considered him a good man, even if his ways were sometimes a mite backward. If you get my drift.

"Well, now, will you look at that," he said as Pardee fumbled in the rest of his pockets for money he must certainly have known by now he didn't have.

I looked up in the direction my deputy was staring and noticed about half a dozen men slowly riding into town.

"Kind of early for visitors, don't you think?" Joshua said in observation.

"With riffraff you never can tell" was the only comment I could think to make at the time. Joshua slowly nodded his head, silently agreeing with my assessment. Most of the men looked as though they'd been riding hard to get someplace, and apparently

Twin Rifles was that place. The trouble was, they looked as though they'd ignored caring for their horses more than themselves while they made their way to our fair town. Not that any of them were dressed in their Sunday-go-to-meeting best, you understand. Hell, most of them had a good three, maybe four days' growth of beard on their scratchy faces.

"Better get yourself some sleep, hoss," I said to my deputy, all but ignoring the strangers who had just ridden into town.

"You betcha, Will," he said and ambled away in that half swagger, half gimpy way he had, heading for the Ferris House and some of Margaret and Rachel Ferris's home cooking. I knew I'd see him back at my office just about the time the bank was fixing to close for the day.

"I'd better git to the bank, Will, before I forget what it was I needed," Pardee Taylor said with a half smile.

I returned the smile and slapped him on the back. "See you later, Pardee." I watched him walk off, but in the back of my mind was the thought of the strangers who had just ridden into town. There was something suspicious about them, something I felt real uneasy about. I determined to check them out, take a quick gander at the wanted posters at my office.

I'd no sooner gotten inside the jail than I heard a gunshot out on the street. By the time I did a quick turn to my rear, I had my Remington .44 in hand and could see that the strangers who had entered Twin Rifles were no longer strangers. From the desperate looks on their faces, not to mention the sacks of what could only have been money, they must have decided to make a friendly withdrawal from our bank. All I needed to see was someone trying to abscond with some of the town's money and you can bet I started taking a real personal interest in them. No, sir, they weren't strangers anymore, not by a long shot!

"Drop it or you're dead, boys!" I yelled at the lot of them. Like a fool, I was standing out in the open, plain as day. I would have shot one or two of them, but Pardee Taylor was dancing between their horses, likely trying to figure out what to do. I was hoping he'd get out of my line of fire, for shooting him wasn't on my mind at the moment. I wanted those yahoos with our money.

All of a sudden guns were going off everywhere. I thought I saw Joshua off to my side down the street, but I was too busy trading shots with the bank robbers to be sure. It only took but two of the shots they were firing in my direction to make me realize that dead heroes don't tell many stories, so I dived behind one of the watering troughs that didn't have a horse tied to it. Nearly all of the robbers had mounted their horses by now, but they were still firing their six-guns at whatever they thought they could hit.

All but one, that is. He had one of the sacks and was carrying it with him, now heading toward the alley that ran along one side of the bank. I took careful aim at him and fired a shot as he rounded the corner, hitting him high in the right shoulder. It must have been his gun hand, for he dropped the weapon he was firing and fell to the ground, more out of fear of being shot again than because of loss of blood, I thought.

The rest of the gang was on its way out of town by now, but that wasn't the end of it. Apparently one of the riders was not only greedy but was also a vengeful son of a bitch. They were riding right past the Ferris House when one of them, who still had a sack in his left hand, along with his reins, drew on Joshua and shot him just as the deputy was taking aim.

Rachel Ferris was in the doorway and let out a scream at the sight of Joshua falling to the ground before her. No sooner had she let out the scream than she was violently pushed to one side and my old pard from the Texas Rangers, Dallas Bodeen, came into full view. He brought his Henry rifle up to his shoulder, aimed at the man who had shot my deputy, and blew him out of his saddle.

"Sorry son of a bitch," I heard his raspy voice growl as he watched the rest of the gang escape after throwing a few more shots in their direction.

"Is he dead?" Rachel was asking, her apron up to her face and covering her mouth as tears ran down her face.

"That son of a bitch?" Dallas said, staring at the lifeless body of the man he had just killed. "Betcherass he is!" Then, realizing he was talking to the woman who had likely just served him his breakfast, he got real humble and said, "Oh, sorry, ma'am. I didn't mean to—"

"It's all right," Rachel said through her tears. "I meant Joshua."

Joshua might have had his ways and been a mite strange on some things, but I couldn't think of anyone in Twin Rifles who disliked the man. Not a soul.

Dallas knelt down beside the deputy and gave him a serious look, as though that alone would determine his health. "He's just fine, Miss Rachel. Looks like he taken one full in the chest, but you ask me this man's too damned tough to die."

"Tough has nothing to do with death, Mr. Bodeen." These words came from Margaret as she brushed past her daughter and pushed Dallas aside. When Dallas gave her an offended look, she added, "Although in your case, I'm sure being *ugly* would keep from bringing on death." She might as well have kicked Dallas Bodeen in his elsewheres.

"Don't you move, mister, or I'll put a hole in you right where you are," I heard Pardee Taylor say in a voice loud enough to be heard all over town. We all turned to look at him and, sure as God made green apples, there he was. He was standing right over the bank robber I'd shot in the arm, the one who'd gone down all too willingly, I thought.

It was then I took a moment to glance around and see almost half of the town in the streets now, all of them armed with some sort of weapon. That must have been all of the gunfire I heard after these yahoos robbed the bank. Of course, you have to realize that the people of Twin Rifles had come that close to losing all of their money not that far back in the past, so who could blame them for showing up in force when the same kind of stunt was pulled again. But that's a whole 'nother canyon.

"Pardee, get him over to the jail and watch him until I get back there," I said to the former town bully. Seeing Pardee act the way he did, not to mention hearing him use those words, why, that was pure amazing.

"He's bleeding, Marshal," Pardee said as he grabbed the outlaw and the man let out a yell.

"I don't care if he bleeds to death, Pardee."

"Good for you, Will," someone in the crowd said, apparently seconding my motion.

"Folks, I appreciate the help," I said, meaning every word I said, "but right now I'd appreciate it if one of you big-time gunmen would put away his pistola and get us the doctor. Joshua's in need of him."

Margaret was doing what she could to comfort Joshua when I knelt down beside him. He had regained consciousness, although I had a notion it would only be briefly.

He tried to smile as he said, "It's gonna be awful hard sitting up nights in this condition."

"You'll do no such thing," Margaret said in what could only have been called a motherly fashion.

But by the time she'd said those words, Joshua had passed out again.

CHAPTER
★ 2 ★

I reckon about half the town spent the next couple of hours fretting over Joshua and just how badly shot he was. Those that weren't fretting were likely praying. Like I said, I couldn't think of a soul in town who disliked the man.

"Won't be long before it's colder than a witch's tit out there," Chance said when he walked into my jail about an hour later. Following him was his brother, George Washington, who went by the nickname G.W., or Wash. For some reason he never did think he looked an awful lot like the father of our country. Both of my boys headed straight for the old Franklin stove and the coffee pot sitting atop it.

"Been too busy to notice it before," I said, keeping

an eye on the man I'd shot, who now sat in the near cell of the jail.

"Say, Pa, what's going on?" Wash asked when his cup was filled with the black stuff. "What's everyone so downtrodden about?"

"Yeah," Chance added. "I ain't seen folks this interested in the dirt since way before the war began. Someone die?"

"One for sure, one almost," I said in a serious tone. "It's the second one the people in this town are concerned about."

"Oh?"

I told the boys about the attempted bank robbery not an hour ago and filled them in on the particulars of what had happened. They sat quietly through the whole telling of it, both grimacing when I mentioned the fact that Joshua had taken a serious hit in the chest.

"Happened right in front of your Rachel," I said to Chance. "Made a scream you could have heard all the way to the Pecos, I swear."

Before I could finish, Chance was on his feet, nearly dropping his cup of coffee, a mean-looking scowl coming quickly to his face. Not that I could blame him, for he and Rachel were known to be serious about their feelings for each other, if you know what I mean. And Chance, well, let's just say that the boy is known for charging head first into trouble before finding out it might be the whole Comanche Nation he was going up against.

"Is she all right?" Those were the first words out of his mouth, and I could tell he wanted a definite answer.

"She's just fine, son," I said with what I hoped was some sort of reassurance. "Old Dallas Bodeen pushed her out of the way and about saved her life, I'd say. You might want to buy the man a beer the next time you see him."

A look of relief came to Chance's face as he said, "I'll do that, Pa. I'll sure do that."

"When's that goddamn sawbones of yours gonna get over here and take a look at me?" the man behind bars said. He'd yet to reveal his name to me, although I'd gone through the wanted posters in my desk and had a fairly good idea of who he might be.

"You don't watch your mouth you're gonna need a dentist, too," I said in my harshest manner. I didn't want this pilgrim to think he was getting off easy. Not on your life!

"Well, damn it, this slug you put in me is painful, mister," he said, coming close to a whine.

"Good. That's why I put it there."

"Who's he?" Chance asked when the man shut up momentarily.

"He ain't saying," I said, tossing a glance the outlaw's way. "But I got him figured for being with the Wells or Forrester Gang, take your pick."

"The Forrester Gang," the outlaw said with a disgusted-looking frown. "Why, I wouldn't be caught dead with a bunch of amateurs like that!"

"Part of the Wells Gang, is that it?" I asked, a hint of a smile appearing on my face. I made sure it did because I wanted the man to know I'd just found out for sure who he was with. After all, no one likes being made a fool of.

"What's it to you?"

"Just want to get the name right on the paperwork," I said. Chance and Wash had the good sense to keep their mouths shut while I did my job and tried to pry one more fact out of this would-be bank robber. "Would you be one of the brothers or one of the gang members, friend?" The Wells Gang had four brothers and three or four other gang members, as I recalled my wanted poster saying.

"Go to hell, lawman."

Being questioned didn't sit pretty with this desperado, that was certain. Or maybe it was the slug that was still in his arm. All I'd done once I'd returned to the office was find an old bandanna and tie it around his wound. I reckon Margaret and the doc would have cussed me something fierce for not making sure it was a clean bandanna, but just between you and me, why, this fellow could have dropped dead and I wouldn't have shed a tear over him. No, sir.

"What are you gonna do with him?" Chance asked. From the look on his face, I thought I could see visions of a rope going through my older boy's mind right then. And he wasn't tossing a loop for one of those longhorns on the Goodnight-Loving Trail, that much I'd bet you.

"Well, that I ain't sure about. Don't seem to me the circuit judge is gonna be around for a couple more months," I said, running a rough hand across my chin, as though the action would produce an answer. "Ary it was up to me, I'd try him here and now, but the folks in this town are a mite prejudiced."

"Can't blame 'em," Wash said, knowing full well how the people in this town felt about losing their money. Hell, he'd had a lot to do with making sure it didn't happen the last time. But like I say, that's a whole 'nother canyon.

Finally I made a decision. "Wash, how'd you like to do some riding for me?" I asked.

"Name it. Ain't much going on now anyway."

"Git over to the Porter Café and have Sarah Ann pack you a lunch of that fried chicken of hers," I said. "Then git your best mount and ride hell-for-leather for San Antonio. Find the telegraph and wire those folks in Austin and see ary this pilgrim has got himself any wants and warrants anywhere else. Being on a wanted poster, I got a notion he and his kind put a lot of miles between them and their last job. I usually have Joshua do this kind of checking for me, but he ain't in the right condition to go right now."

"Give me three, four days at the most and I'll be back," Wash said as he headed for the door.

"And Wash?"

He stopped, his hand on the door as he prepared to leave. "Yeah?"

"Find out when they can get a judge down here to try this son of a bitch."

"I understand."

"Best stop by Kelly's Hardware and pick up some more ammunition," Chance added. I reckon that was his own way of looking after his brother. "Might pick up a second pistol, too."

Wash nodded and was gone.

"Where's that goddamn sawbones?" my resident outlaw all but yelled. It was easy to see the bullet was really bothering him.

Chance pulled out his bowie knife and tested the edge of it. With a smile that was more of a leer, he said, "Why don't you put a mite of wood in that Franklin of yours, Pa? Hell, I'll pull the damned bullet out of him."

The outlaw could see right away the only one who would have any fun doing that was Chance. But that's how my son is. "Now, wait a minute," the robber said, all of a sudden mighty hesitant about being treated. "I said I wanted the doctor."

"No, you didn't," Chance said with a smile. "You was complaining about that bullet in your arm." He held up his knife again, the leer more prominent now. "And Dr. Bowie is gonna take care of you."

"Git your shirt off, sonny," I said in a stern manner. "I never did like complainers."

It didn't take Chance but fifteen minutes to find that slug of mine and pull it out. I could only figure that it had struck part of the man's bone somewhere. Otherwise I might have been lucky and it would have passed through the arm and gone on into his heart. Then all I would have had to deal with was a corpse instead of some flannelmouth.

"Better cauterize it, don't you think?" Chance asked me when he was through.

"What are you asking *him* for? I'm the one who's been shot!" the outlaw complained.

"He'll likely bleed to death or die of infection ary you don't," I agreed.

"Now wait a minute . . ."

But the man had no say in it and did nothing but sweat something fierce as Chance stuck his bowie knife inside the Franklin stove for a minute or so. It was enough time for this hombre to work up his tough.

"Ain't much of a talker, is that it?" I asked.

"Like I said, lawman, go to hell."

Chance heard the man's comment and slapped the side of that hot knife up against the flannelmouth's arm as soon as he was within range. It caught the outlaw by surprise, and he let out a bloodcurdling scream not unlike the one I'd heard Rachel give off earlier. Me, I held my breath as he did so, for the smell of burning flesh has never been one of my favorite odors, if you get my drift.

"Think it'll do?" Chance asked, admiring his handiwork.

"That depends."

I looked at the outlaw, who suddenly didn't seem so tough. But he must have wanted to play it to the hilt and growled, "Go to hell."

"I think it needs another one, Chance. Yes, sir, another one."

The man's eyes were about ready to fall out of his head when he saw Chance headed back toward the Franklin stove.

"No!"

Tough, my ass!

"Now then, what did you say your name was, sonny?"

A look of relief ran across his face, and I knew he had reached a point where he didn't care one damn bit about being as tough as nails.

"Wells," he said. "Bob Wells."

CHAPTER

★ 3 ★

It was three long days before Wash made it back from San Antonio. I say long because with each passing day I could see the hatred in the townspeople growing. Not that you could blame them. Once the doctor had gotten through pulling that piece of lead out of Joshua's chest, he had pronounced the man alive but barely. My deputy remained in the doctor's back room, a couple of women in town volunteering to take turns watching over him as he fought his way back to health. I reckon those women who had passed on their pitiful feelings for the man, which likely explained the ugliness I was seeing in the people as they passed by my jail. Like I said, the folks in this town had taken a real liking to Joshua.

"I don't think I been this tended to since Mama

tooken care of me in my youth," Joshua said with a flush to his face about the second day, when I visited him.

"Oh, nonsense," Sarah Ann said as she spoon-fed him what smelled to be some sort of broth. She'd been one of the first to volunteer once she heard about Joshua's condition. "Wash ain't here to feed supper to, being on a deed for the marshal and all."

"What about Chance?" my deputy said in a worried tone. "Don't you have to feed him?"

"Let him fend for himself for once," she said with a smile, spooning some more broth into him. "Besides, he's had it real good since me and Wash got hitched."

Through the pain he must have still felt, Joshua managed a smile. "Yeah, that boy can surely put away some vittles, I'll give him that."

"Don't let her fool you, Joshua," I said with a straight face. "She knows he likes his food. Why, all she's doing is making sure Chance stops by the Ferris House for his evening meal. Trying to get him to court Rachel, is what she's doing," I added with a wink and a nod.

"Oh, go on, Marshal," she said, a red flush coming to her face as she spoke.

Maybe she knew I was likely right in my specula-tions. Hell, if there was one thing I'd found out in all these years it was that women could be devious, especially when they were helping one another plot on how to get a man cornered and snared.

To Sarah Ann I said, "And you stop calling me Marshal. Will is just fine."

An impish smile came to her as she said, "All right, Papa Will."

"Well, now, don't go making me feel *too* old, woman."

It was on the third day that things got a mite touchy concerning Bob Wells and his stay at my jail. For being the fall season I was looking for it to cool off a good deal, but it was one of those days when the sun had different ideas altogether. By three that afternoon I'd had more than my fill of coffee for the day. Not that it was making me nervous or anything, you understand. It was just that I'd been getting some strange looks throughout the day, looks that were anything but friendly, which was odd for people I normally called my friends.

I suppose when I tell it to my grandchildren I'll likely embellish the story a mite and tell them that it was all the fault of the sun that day. Being a city person has several drawbacks, I've found. One is that when you spend most of your time in the shade, why, the sun just drives you off the streets as soon as you get out on them. That leads to one of the other drawbacks, meaning that when a man decides to find a haven from the heat, it's usually the local watering hole, which was where I headed. Ernie Johnson's saloon being the only one in town, why, he tends to get a lot more business in the summertime than he will in the winter. Which is likely where it all started. After all, men talk.

"Will! Will Carston! Are you in there?" I heard a voice shatter the peace and quiet of the afternoon that day. I'd been sitting there waiting for Joshua to show up, knowing in the back of my mind that it would be a while before he did, when they came.

18

I opened the door, only to see a couple dozen of the citizens of Twin Rifles standing in the street before me.

"Sure, I'm here. What can I do for you, George?" I said to the one I thought I'd heard talking. A quick glance at the lot of them told me they'd been mulling something over and doing it together, probably over at Ernie's. Sweat was starting to break out on George Hansom's face. But being short and stout the way he was, it could have been there since he'd gotten out of bed.

"We been talking things over, Will," he said, trying to sound a mite braver than he had to, I thought.

I gave my head a slow nod. "That's what I thought. Had a few drinks along the way, too, I'd bet."

"What of it?"

"What's on your mind, George?"

"It's that outlaw in jail."

"Figures." I said the word almost under my breath, as though talking to myself.

"We figure he's a killer."

"You're likely right, George. But we don't know that for sure. At least, if he is, he ain't saying so to me."

"Well, we want him, Will. And now." George Hansom was trying to sound courageous as all get-out. Too bad his wife wasn't here to see him, for she would have been the only one he'd have impressed.

"Now, George, you know I can't do that." I scratched the back of my head, using the motion as a delay. Finally I stuck with the truth. "You know, boys, normally I'd tell you to go back to Ernie's and have a beer on me. But I've got a notion you've likely already had one too many. So why don't you just go home?

19

Besides, you know I ain't got room in this jail for all of you."

I wasn't about to see who wanted to debate the matter and simply turned around and went back into the jail. I gave the crowd a glance as I crossed by the front window and saw them dispersing, just as I'd told them to.

Fifteen minutes later they were back. They were pretty vocal about it, too. A rock crashed through the window, sending glass flying every which way. I already had my Remington on, so barging straight through that door was no problem if wanting to see me was what the men were after.

George Hansom was a mite more red-eyed and staggering. But it was the pistol he held in his hand that made him look dangerous to me. The coiled rope in his other hand didn't make him look any less tame. A quick gander at the same two dozen that had appeared before me a few minutes ago and I could see they nearly all had rifles or six-guns.

"We mean business, Will!" George said in his most forceful manner.

"I don't know about business, George, but you're damn sure gonna get a bill if you're the one who broke the glass out of my window," I said in a stern manner. "Do you know how much that glass cost? Come all the way from St. Louis, it did."

"Will, that son of a bitch don't need a trial; he needs a hanging." Even with the slight slur in his voice, I could see the man was determined.

"Couldn't agree with you more, George. But you folks hired me to preserve the order, and part of the order says he gets a trial *before* he gets the hanging."

"I ain't gonna say it again, Will." This time George

Hansom had his six-gun pointed at my belly by the time his words were out.

"Serious, are you?" I tried to sound like I wasn't scared of him at all, and most of the time I wasn't. But I don't mind telling you, hoss, that the business end of that six-shooter plumb scared me to death.

"Damn right." The gun didn't move, still aimed at my gut.

"You sure you want to do that?"

Before he could answer, a gunshot filled the air, one that got all of our attention. Every man jack in that lynch mob turned around, for it had come from their rear. I reckon what they saw surprised them.

Pardee Taylor stood on the boardwalk across the street from me, his six-gun in hand. He had as serious a look about him as I'd seen on him the other day when he drew on Bob Wells.

"Believe me, you don't want to do that," he said. The words sounded a mite different from the look the man wore. In fact, I could have sworn they had a good deal of fear in them. But Pardee didn't have to worry about acting tough, although I was grateful for the way he'd diverted this bunch.

Another diversion took place just then as Wash came riding down the street and pulled up in front of my office. Or maybe I should say right next to the mob. Wash has always picked up on things real quick, so he only had to take one glance at this group with all their weapons facing me to know what he had to do next.

"Well, now, looks like I come to the party just in time," he said as he slid off his mount, his Dance Brothers revolver in one hand. "What's going on, Pa?"

"They got a mite liquored up and decided to do something about the local jail population," I said.

"I see." Wash moved over beside me on the boardwalk. I still had my Remington in my holster, but Wash had that Dance Brothers revolver of his ready for use. "You know, I never did shoot a friend. Of course, if you go after Pa, you won't be my friends no more, so I reckon it won't be hard shooting you after all."

"George, you and your compadres are drunk," I said in a forceful way. I could be businesslike, too, if that was the game they were playing. "Now, *I'm not gonna tell you again!* Git on home or I'll do you all in!"

Past experience had taught me that once you cut the head off a rattlesnake, he'll pretty well die on his own. The same is true of most lynch mobs. If I'd had my Remington out, I'd have had to put it away or crack George's skull wide open. Since I didn't, I had surprise on my side. And being a rather big man in stature, I found it easy to take one quick step down off that boardwalk and knock George flat on his ass.

"Any other takers?" I snarled, looking among the crowd for someone else who thought he was froggy enough to fight.

There wasn't.

"You didn't have to do that," George said, good and sober now.

"The hell I didn't!"

"If he didn't, I would have, George, no matter how much older than me you are," Wash said in an even tone. "Besides, Pa couldn't try that outlaw here if he wanted to."

Suddenly we had another diversion, one that even got my attention.

"Oh?" George and I said together.

"Turns out the fella you got in the hoosegow is a killer and a bank robber, Pa."

"Do tell." I was finally hearing something of interest this afternoon.

"Seems there's extradition papers on the man for some killing he and his gang did up around Fort Dodge," Wash said, pulling some papers out of his saddlebags and handing them to me.

I undid the deerskin and glanced over the papers. True enough, they were extradition papers for Bob Wells for just the reason Wash had given.

"Read 'em yourself if you're sober enough, George," I said and handed them to the man.

He did the same quick reading I had and handed them back. "I still say he needs hanging."

"And I still say there's an order to all of it, and it looks like this is the order, George," I said, holding the paper up for all to see.

That did it, and they were soon gone as quickly as they had appeared. As they left, I called Pardee Taylor over to me.

"Want to thank you for stepping in when you did, Pardee," I said, holding out my hand to him. "That took guts."

Pardee shrugged. "Ernie told me to go get Chance, said it looked like you was in trouble. By the time I was out the batwings, it looked like trouble had already found you."

Then Pardee was gone, too.

"Come on, son," I said, slapping Wash on the back in a friendly manner. "Won't be long before Big

John's got his evening menu out, and I reckon you'll want to see Sarah Ann."

"You bet."

"Got to make one stop first, though."

"What's that?"

"Need to check on the next stage coming through for Fort Dodge."

CHAPTER
★ 4 ★

I visited Joshua one more time that day and was gladly informed that the doctor had just paid the patient a call and proclaimed him on the road to recovery.

"Good," I said with what had to be the happiest smile I'd spread on my face in some time. "I'm still needing a deputy, you know."

It almost seemed like the wrong thing to say, because Joshua started getting sorrowful about the way he'd gotten shot up and all, thinking it was all his fault. But I put a halt to that right quick and told him to get to his recovering, for I planned on being gone the next day and likely for a week or two to come.

"Checked with old Harley at the freight office and

found out the stage for Fort Dodge is coming through tomorrow about noon," I explained, then proceeded to tell my deputy about the extradition papers Wash had brought back on Bob Wells for some killing he'd done up around Fort Dodge.

"A bad one, is he?" Joshua asked.

"Well, he thinks he is, but I've got other notions about that, hoss" was my reply.

"Oh, you won't let him git the best of you. I know you better than that, Will." Joshua raised his arm and gave me a slap on the knee to let me know he had confidence in me and my ability as the lawman of Twin Rifles. Or maybe he was just showing that he'd gotten a sight better than I might have thought, considering the way the man looked, which was still a mite sickly.

"I know, Joshua." There is something about giving Joshua a wink and a nod that has always served to back up anything I've told the man over the few short years I've known him. But then I reckon that's how some folks communicate with one another. "You just get better and see can you be wearing that deputy's badge by the time I make it back. Just make sure you do what the doctor tells you, you hear?"

"You bet, Will."

"I'll see ary I can drop by to see you tomorrow morning before I have to leave."

He said that would be fine, and I left, knowing that as much as he wanted to palaver, he was likely needing his rest more.

If it hadn't been for Margaret Ferris, why, I doubt that a stage line would have had anything to do with a town as small as Twin Rifles. But rather than build its own relay station about two miles north of Twin

Rifles, the stage line sent its coaches south off the trail from the west and right through town. They did that because the head of the stage line had discovered that Margaret Ferris not only ran a boarding house but made some of the best stew this side of heaven. Being a man of money-saving ways, the head of the line decided to kill two birds with one stone, as they say. He not only gave his crew time to drop off any mail for our fair town and change teams but offered them and the passengers a chance at dining at noon on some of Margaret's mouth-watering stew. I couldn't recall Margaret ever forgetting when that stage was coming through, either. Step off that stage and you could count on having a heaping plate of that stew, and it didn't matter whether there were eight passengers or only one. There was always plenty for all.

I stopped by to see Joshua the next morning, just like I'd said. I'd chosen my black broadcloth Sunday-go-to-meeting coat with a clean white shirt and a string tie, the one I usually only wore on special occasions. The sight of me in it seemed to confuse Joshua, for the first thing out of his mouth was "Where's the Sunday social at, Will?"

I smiled and explained to him that these were also my traveling clothes. Hell, I was a representative of Twin Rifles, wasn't I? Had to look my best to give a good accounting of myself and all.

I had Bob Wells seated at Margaret Ferris's community table about fifteen minutes before the stage was due in, giving him the stern admonition that if he tried anything funny, why, he'd never do it a second time. He sat real quiet after those words. Made him think, I reckon.

Actually, Bob Wells was real peaceful compared to

what took place once the stage pulled up outside. Even inside the Ferris House, I could recognize old Black-snake Hank's gravelly voice whenever the stage came through town. As I recall, you could just about set your watch by the time he came through, too. Seldom more than five minutes off, one way or another, and as close to being on time as anyone I've ever seen who drove a stage.

"If you want to get off right here, ma'am, I'll get this team changed and see can I make it back in time to get me a few bites of Miss Margaret's stew," I heard Hank say as he opened the creaky side door to the stage-coach.

For a moment I had a worrisome thought, especially if the woman who was getting off the stage was going to be traveling with me and my prisoner on the rest of the trip to Fort Dodge. Mind you, women could be a pleasurable species to have out on this frontier, but I'd learned long ago that they could be just as much a bother as a pleasure. All it took was the wrong circumstances and they could ruin everything for you. Yes, sir.

Apparently Margaret hit it off fine with the woman who'd just gotten off the stage, although I couldn't hear a word of their conversation until they came through the entrance to the boarding house. You can't hear spit when a stagecoach or anything attached to it—like a six-horse hitch—is anywhere in the area. And that includes two women talking away about this, that, and the other, especially when they haven't had a chance to palaver with another woman in some time.

She looked more Rachel's age than Margaret's, this woman who entered the Ferris House. Dark eyes and a dark shade of brown hair, if that's possible. She stood as tall as Margaret, which is saying something, and had the high cheekbones you'd expect to find on an Indian. But she didn't look all that much like an Indian. Oh, she had a dark complexion all right, but I'd say she was closer to being of Mexican ancestry than Indian. If the first words I heard her speak were any indication, she spoke perfect English. Better than me, anyway.

She had a full dress on, which has always mystified me. Not the dress itself, you understand, for most women would wear one when called upon to dress up. It's just that I'd always suspicioned that those big thick dresses had to be the equivalent of an old mountain man wearing a buffalo robe or a bear skin in the middle of summer on the hottest, driest desert you could imagine on earth—and I've been on a couple of those. That dress was also why Margaret seated this woman at the end of the community table, women not showing so much as an ankle in those days.

"Gentlemen, this is Miss Catherine Innes," Margaret said by way of introduction as the young lady took her seat.

"Pleasure to meet you, ma'am," I said, only half standing up from my seat at the community table.

"Mine as well, sir," Catherine Innes said with a polite nod of her head.

Bob Wells didn't say a thing. Either he was a rude bastard or he was taking real seriously my advice about keeping his mouth shut and not saying or doing anything.

"Plan on staying in Twin Rifles or just passing through?" I asked when Margaret had left the room to fetch her pot of stew.

"Oh, just passing through, sir," she said with a

29

pleasant smile that showed a mite of red on her cheeks.

"I'm Marshal Will Carston, ma'am. Pleased to meet you. I'll be riding herd on this feller next to me on this trip," I said, nodding toward Bob Wells, who was handcuffed even as he ate. "Going to Fort Dodge, he is. I'd stay away from him if I was you."

"My, he certainly doesn't look dangerous," she said as she looked at him.

"Looks don't mean nothing out here, ma'am," I said. "Some of those baby-faced children of ours went off to war and came back with hearts as cold as a winter's night. No ma'am, looks don't mean much out here. Except on a woman, of course. And on you I'd say they go right fine."

"Don't pay no never mind to the marshal," Margaret said as she reentered the dining room and began spooning stew onto our plates. "He thinks he's a flirt when it comes to looking at pretty women." Her words sounded as though she'd spoken in jest, but I could tell when she got around to filling my plate that the look on her face didn't have a bit of humor in it. Not one bit. In fact, I'd near guarantee that if she'd had a straight razor in her hand, why, she'd as likely have cut my throat as shaved me. Like I said, sometimes women can be a bother to a man. If you know what I mean.

The conversation sort of dried up then, and we made eating the meal on our plates a serious matter. I thought I saw the woman give me what I thought to be a coy look, which sort of confused me, for I was old enough to be her father a couple of times over if she was the age of Sarah Ann Porter, my newfound daughter-in-law. Hell, Sarah Ann was only eighteen!

Still, there's no accounting for the way a woman's mind works. I'd learned that a long time back.

Bob Wells didn't make any trouble as we ate, but I swear that every time young Catherine Innes looked my way, I saw Margaret Ferris standing off to the side, big black coffee pot in hand, looking like she was about to pour the contents on top of my head. Why, you'd think I was the one who was urging this young lady to make those looks.

Blacksnake Hank finally made his way through the doors, much to my relief. With no one there but the four of us, why, I was expecting Margaret to do something rash at any minute. At least heading back into the kitchen gave her something to do besides stand there and glare at me.

Hank was a tall, skinny man who must have come close to getting his bones broken up a time or two, the way he jostled around on the top seat of that stagecoach. I had yet to see him clean-shaven, always looking as though he had a three- or four-day growth of beard, sort of like a man who was trying to decide whether or not he really wanted to go on growing a full beard. Normally, Hank could be a talkative type, but not when food was put before the man. Like the rest of us, he knew it would likely be a long while before his next decent meal, so it was best to make a small feast out of the one before him now.

"Parfect, Miss Margaret," Hank said when he was through. "Just parfect." He wiped his sleeve across his face, taking with it any mess he might have made on his mustache while eating. "Now, Miss Margaret, I don't suppose . . ."

But before the man could finish, Margaret had produced what looked like a small flour sack, but it

31

didn't smell anything like flour. This had gotten to be a ritual with Margaret and Blacksnake Hank, wherein she gave the stagecoach driver a sack full of her fresh-made biscuits. To anyone else this might have looked like an act of kindness, but those of us who'd known Hank and Margaret any length of time knew it was no more than a trade-off. Hank got a sack of mighty good-tasting biscuits to last him the rest of the trip. In return, he would also accept from Margaret a list of items that were not available locally. The stagecoach driver would later pick them up and deliver them to her the next time he passed through. Both thought it a fair trade and made no complaints about it.

"Thank you, Miss Margaret," Hank said with a smile that gave off pure pleasure, even on an ugly face like Blacksnake Hank's. "I really appreciate it."

"It's my pleasure, Hank."

"Well, folks, time to git, I reckon," Hank said to us as he headed for the stagecoach he'd left out front.

"That's an excellent stew, ma'am," Catherine Innes said as she rose from the table. "Could I have—"

"It was nice meeting you, too, dearie," Margaret Ferris said, suddenly turning into a witch. She had the young woman's elbow and was quickly guiding her toward the door before she could say anything else.

As soon as Catherine Innes was out the door, Margaret turned to me, a frown on her face. "You and I have to talk," she said, reminding me a lot of my mother when she put her stern face on.

"What about this feller?" I asked, motioning toward Bob Wells.

"Say, Marshal . . ." It was Blacksnake Hank, sticking his head back in the door, itchy to go, itchy to be on time.

"Hank, pull your six-gun out, stick it in this fellow's back, and find him a seat on your coach," Margaret said, all authority.

"Yes, ma'am." Hank did just as she told him and soon both men were out of the room.

"Maybe I should make you my deputy while I'm gone," I said, trying to keep a straight face. "That way Chance can go back to breaking horses and by the time I get back you'll have a reputation for skilleting to death anyone who crosses your path."

"Oh, shut up, you fool" was all she said before taking my face in both hands and giving me one hellacious kiss. This woman meant business! Me, I did just what she said.

"Will Carston, you be careful," she said when our lips parted. The frown had gone from her face now, replaced by a worried look. And the worry was meant for me, that much I knew.

"Don't you worry, darlin'," I said, trying to sound encouraging. "I've handled men like Bob Wells before."

I broke away quick, hearing Hank give one final "All aboard!" yell outside. I was almost to the door when I heard Margaret say her parting words to me. Trouble was I wasn't at all sure if I heard the words right.

It sounded like she said, "It ain't the outlaw I'm worried about."

CHAPTER

★ 5 ★

Afternoon, Miss Margaret," Pardee Taylor said, tipping his hat as Margaret watched the stagecoach leave Twin Rifles. She had rushed out of the Ferris House after Will left, not knowing what it was she wanted to say, but rushing after him just the same. She'd been too late. Old Blacksnake Hank was cracking his whip over the heads of his six-horse hitch and raising a heap of dust as she made her way to the boardwalk in front of the Ferris House. She didn't even hear Pardee Taylor approach and greet her. Not until he'd repeated his words.

"Oh, hello, Mr. Taylor," she said, still watching the stagecoach leaving in a ball of dust. It would have been evident to anyone watching the woman that she'd spoken out of habit rather than in a purely honest attempt at greeting a customer. But then, the folks in Twin Rifles, except for Ernie Johnson, didn't treat Pardee Taylor like a customer for much of anything. When the stagecoach had disappeared from sight, Margaret Ferris regained her sense and turned to Pardee, looking businesslike. "What is it I can do for you, Mr. Taylor?"

"Seeing the marshal off, were you, ma'am?" Pardee said with a knowing smile.

It was the kind of smile Margaret didn't like on men like Pardee, although she really was sweet on Will Carston. Not that she'd have admitted it, unless somebody forced her to. Margaret Ferris didn't like liars any better than Will Carston did.

The look on her face didn't change at all as she said, "As a matter of fact, I *was* seeing Marshal Carston off. Not that it's any of your business."

Without waiting for an answer or any other type of conversation with the man, Margaret went back inside the Ferris House, silently hoping that if she ignored Pardee he would go away. But she knew the hope was futile as she heard the heavy clomp of his feet behind her, following her toward the kitchen.

"I suppose you've come to see about begging a meal off of me," she said without turning to face the man, not once breaking stride as she entered the kitchen.

"Well, now that you mention it, that does smell like your stew, Miss Margaret," Pardee said, sniffing the delicious aroma of the kitchen, a smell that seemed to be a constant presence whenever the Ferris women were cooking up a meal, which was pretty near all day every day. Clearing his throat, Pardee tried to sound the way he thought a good, upstanding citizen of Twin Rifles ought to sound. Maybe a man like Will Carston, whom he'd come to admire of late. He quickly grabbed the dusty hat off his head and said, "But I ain't a-begging for it. No, ma'am."

"You're not?" The man before her might as well have hit Margaret Ferris, his words jolted her that much. "Well, Mr. Taylor, I will admit, that'll be a change, and a definite change for the good, I might add."

Pardee's voice suddenly lost its manliness as he said in a humble manner, "I'm afraid I ain't got no money to pay for it, though."

"Well, then, that takes care of that, doesn't it?" Margaret said in disgust. "You're right back to begging, and I can't afford to go handing free food out to everyone who comes along, you know." She didn't mention the sack full of biscuits she'd just handed to Blacksnake Hank, figuring that was an altogether different matter.

Her words hurt Pardee, but they also made him angry. Hell, everyone in this damned town had treated him like so much cow droppings ever since he'd gotten sober and done his damnedest to stay that way. Then he remembered Will Carston telling him it would be a hard row to hoe, then slapping him on the back and encouraging him to do his best, no matter what people said. Well, by God, he'd show them! He'd show them all!

"Begging your pardon, ma'am," he said, cocking an eyebrow and sticking his head out at the woman before him, "but I *ain't* a beggar and I *ain't* begging."

"Pardee Taylor, I'm about a hand's reach from a good solid rolling pin, so you'd better watch your words," Margaret said in defense of herself.

"Damn it, Chance is right!" Pardee said with a

scowl. "All you women do is gab and palaver and never give a man a chance to get a word in edgewise. Why, no wonder the man's a confirmed bachelor!"

"What!" The response was a surprise to both Pardee and Margaret, for it came from Rachel, who had been standing quietly off to the side, stirring the stew and gathering some plates for the guests out front.

"Ma'am?"

"Chance Carston said that about women, did he?" By the time Rachel's words were out, she had quickly made her way to her mother's side. Pardee decided that, hands on hips like she was standing, she looked an awful lot like her mother.

"Oh, Miss Rachel, don't you go a-telling Chance I was the one who said that, now," Pardee said, a sudden fear in his voice. "Why, Chance would never talk to me again. Yes, ma'am."

Rachel Ferris was untying her apron as she said, "By the time I get through with him, Chance Carston may never speak to me again, either!"

"Now, Rachel, you just calm down and put that apron back on," Margaret said in a stern motherly voice. "Giving Chance a piece of your mind is going to have to wait. Right now we've got to get ready to serve a decent helping of stew to the next customers we get in the dining room. Now, git! Git!" she added, shooing her daughter off with the motion of a hand.

"Yes, Mother," Rachel said as she turned to go back to the stew pot, but she didn't sound anything like a submissive daughter when she spoke the words.

"Just how do you plan on getting some of my stew, Mr. Taylor?" Margaret asked in a superior tone. She'd quickly formed the opinion that it was better to take

37

the upper hand with men like Pardee than to let them go babbling on. The trouble was, it could be awful hard acting superior to a big brute like Pardee Taylor, who was indeed a big man, almost as big as Will and his boys.

"Seems simple enough to me, Miss Margaret."

"Oh?" Trying to imagine how Will would have talked to this man, she added, "Do tell."

"With the marshal gone for a while, I reckon you'll be needing someone to chop your firewood."

Margaret had been so distracted by Will and the young woman known as Catherine Innes that she'd clean forgotten that very evident fact. Will Carston had been staying in a room at the Ferris House for a couple of years now. Rather than charge him her daily rate, Margaret had worked out a barter situation where Will would chop some wood in the morning and she'd provide his room and board and a couple of meals a day. It had proved to be an amiable arrangement for both of them. But Pardee Taylor was right; with Will gone for a week or two, she hadn't planned on what she'd do about the supply of firewood she needed daily. After all, she and Rachel did prepare three good-sized meals each day.

"As a matter of fact, I will need someone to take care of my firewood supply, now that you mention it," she said, her demeanor now back to that of a civilized businesswoman.

"If you can see your way to feeding me at least twice a day, ma'am, I can chop you a right smart amount of kindling," Pardee said with a bit of pride.

"All right, Mr. Taylor," Margaret said with a proffered hand and the smile of a businesswoman. "You've got yourself a deal, but on two conditions."

"Name 'em," Pardee said as he took her small hand in his rather large fist.

"You start this afternoon—after I feed you, of course—and you eat your meals in the kitchen." To herself in a lower voice, she added, "I don't want to scare away the customers."

But Pardee didn't hear it, only pumped her hand up and down like a water pump gone dry. "You won't regret it, Miss Margaret. I swear you won't. Thanks, I really appreciate it."

"I'm sure, Mr. Taylor," Margaret said. "Rachel, get one of your bigger bowls—"

"I know, Mama, I know," Rachel said. Heading toward the item she was looking for, she added, "There won't be no stew left over today. No, sir."

Pardee Taylor plunked himself down at the one and only table that was vacant in the entire kitchen area and set his hat on the chair next to him.

"Ladies," he said with a smile, happy about his new job, "why don't you all just call me Pardee?" It was an honest attempt to be friendly.

"Certainly, Mr. Taylor," Margaret Ferris said and was gone from the kitchen, a tureen of stew in her possession.

The Ferris women managed to feed all of their customers and even give Pardee Taylor a second helping of leftover stew before they could take a breather and stand just outside the kitchen door. It was here that they managed to catch up on their small talk.

"I sure hope Will takes care of himself," Margaret said to her daughter.

"Don't worry, Mama. Marshal Will can take care of himself. You know that."

"I was talking about that woman, that Catherine Innes, when I said it, dear," Margaret added by way of explanation. "I've got a strange feeling he's going to get in some kind of trouble over that woman."

"Nonsense, Mama," Rachel said, trying to be cheerful about the whole subject, yet knowing how much Will Carston really meant to her mother. "How could anything happen? It's just a stagecoach ride."

"That may be, honey, but I guess you didn't see the way that woman was looking at Will while they were eating. I tell you, there's trouble about."

Rachel frowned, trying to picture in her mind what she imagined her mother to be talking about. "Are you sure?"

"You bet I am," Margaret said stubbornly. "Didn't you see the way she was giving him those smiling stares?"

Rachel was silent a moment, thinking back to the earlier meal. Then, shaking her head, she said to her mother, "No. You're wrong. That Catherine whatever-her-name-is wasn't looking at Will. She was looking at the other man, the one next to Will. You know, that prisoner he's taking up to Fort Dodge. Bob Wells? Is that his name?"

Inside the kitchen, Pardee Taylor heard parts of the discussion the women had but paid little attention, picking up only snatches of talk here and there. Chance was right, he thought to himself, all a woman will do is talk and talk and talk. Most of it hardly made any sense at all.

CHAPTER
★ 6 ★

The railroads hadn't come to Texas yet, although I'd been hearing a lot about that big transcontinental line they were building from San Francisco to St. Louis. Passed the legislation for it back in '63 or so, as I recall, but hadn't gotten a good start on things until after the war was over. Get a couple of railroad men together and they'd swear to you that your state—or territory, whichever the case may be—would be the very next one to be invaded by the Iron Horse, as they liked to call that big beast that moved on rails.

Until such time as the railroads came to Texas, there were only a handful of methods for getting around. And the stagecoach was one of them. Not that we were all that backward, you understand. Why, we'd had upwards of thirty-some different stagecoach lines back around 1860, just before the war began. Nothing as big as that Butterfield line—or the Jackass Express, the nickname they'd given the San Antonio–San Diego Line back when it started out in the early 1850s. Hell, son, what else would you call an outfit that used jackasses to get from San Antonio to San Diego and delivered the U.S. mail in just shy of a month's time? Believe me, no other nickname seemed to fit.

Out of those thirty-some stagecoach lines, sixteen were owned and controlled by the firm of Sawyer, Risher and Hall. With names like that you'd think it was a bunch of lawyers getting together to palaver, but it wasn't. For running a bunch of small stagecoach lines, most of them only running to three or four cities or towns in one particular region, these fellows did an awful lot of mail contracting. Why, I'd read someplace they were supposed to be the biggest mail contractors in the whole United States of these Americas! And that's big! They employed some three hundred men and had over one thousand mules and horses. Ran their lines into Louisiana, too, not just Texas. But that's getting petty.

Old Blacksnake Hank had his reins in firm control as we rolled out of Twin Rifles in that Concord coach. You could only fit five or six people in one of those coaches, so any more of us and it would have been a tight squeeze for someone. Granted, there was only the three of us, but like I said, this Catherine Innes had on a real full dress, and it took up near all of the side of the coach she was sitting on. Made me glad I wasn't a woman, looking at that damn thing all spread out like it was.

On the other hand, taking a gander at Catherine

Innes, well, I'd have to admit that it, too, made me glad I was a man. I'd made sure not to pay much attention to her at the community table, Margaret being there and looking on like she was.

I'd grown to like Margaret a lot in the past two decades, and we'd become good friends, just as my wife had become good friends with her husband. But then our respective spouses had died and I'd come to see Margaret in a whole different light the last two years or so, now that we were both without a spouse. However, I'd known better than to make any advances toward her, my wife being gone only those two years. Grieving and all, you know.

Seeing this young woman across from me now, well, it brought out something in me that said I'd grieved long enough. Maybe it was noticing the real beauty of her as she sat there, looking out the window at the passing plains. I had a good glimpse of her face in profile, well defined and sharp featured, especially the cheekbones. From where I sat I could see they were high on her face, and I'd have to admit they gave her a genuine beauty. A real looker, as Chance would put it.

We rode nearly five miles in silence, I'd gauge, me looking at Catherine Innes and trying to find something about her that might remind me of Cora, my one and only wife. Catherine Innes was just looking innocently out the window at the world going by her. As for Bob Wells, I had to give him a glance every once in a while just to make sure he wasn't trying any funny tricks, but for the most part I reckon he stayed pretty quiet. But why not? It was a long ride to Fort Dodge, and he had plenty of time to try to pull something on me . . . something I knew he'd do. It being just a matter of time and all.

We couldn't have gone much farther than those five miles when I heard Hank cussing louder than normal, then felt the coach come to a halt as he whoa-ed down the six-horse hitch.

"Aw, hell," I muttered as I saw the reason for the stop. "Begging your pardon, ma'am," I added as I stepped over her dress as best I could, opened the door, and got out of the coach.

"Shoulda knowed that feller would bring out the worst in your town, Marshal," Hank said, still sitting atop his box seat, as calm as could be. The only thing that didn't seem calm, other than the look on his face, was the sawed-off double-barreled shotgun he had draped across the crook of his arm. And he had it pointing right at the dozen or so horsemen who'd pulled up on my side of the stagecoach.

"You recognize 'em, too, huh?" I said, taking in the whole bunch of them, most of them being the same men I'd had a run-in with in town over whether Bob Wells would get lynched or not.

"Shoot, hoss, it ain't hard to spot a fool."

"Know what you mean, Hank. Know what you mean."

"Carny? Wilson? Being sociable these days, are you?" Two of the Hadley brothers were the only strangers to this crowd. Both men were big and strong and tough. And loud. They never had liked me or my boys, and some time back the big lugs had started a fight with us in the Porter Café. But it was all five Hadley brothers then. I'll admit that me and my boys got our knuckles scraped some, but those Hadleys, why, they fared a lot worse for wear than we did. But that's a whole 'nother canyon, if you get my drift.

"Just come along for some excitement, Marshal,"

Carny Hadley snarled. You might say it was how the man talked normally. Piss-ugly mean and had looks to go with it to boot. These two would never have to worry about wives, for I couldn't fashion any woman desperate enough to go after either of them.

"You come to the right place, boys," Hank said with a sneer of his own and cocked one of the barrels of his shotgun.

"Actually, you've come to the wrong place," I said, correcting the stagecoach driver. Maybe Blacksnake Hank was itching for a fight, but I just wanted to get my prisoner through to Fort Dodge safe and sound. "I'm just taking a prisoner with me, and I don't want no trouble. Now, the lot of you turn them horses about and git on back to Twin Rifles."

I've got to admit to you, friend, that I wasn't feeling all that comfortable at the moment, and the heat of the day had nothing whatsoever to do with it. It was that damned broadcloth suit of mine. It was a whole lot tighter than the normal everyday clothes I wore, and I knew it would slow me down trying to draw my Remington on these yahoos. And that made me feel real uneasy about this whole affair. "Besides, I've got a lady inside, and you wouldn't want getting her hurt on your minds, would you?"

"Won't do you a bit of good, Marshal," Hank said, still eager as hell for a fight. "These fellers come to dance and they ain't even off their hosses yet."

"And what are you gonna do about it, old man?" This time it was Wilson Hadley who spoke up. It almost seemed as though they had elected themselves spokesmen for the group.

"Why, I was thinking of helping you outta them saddles, I was," Hank said, proving he could trade

45

insults with the best of them. Not that the Hadley brothers were all that good at insults, you understand. They just said dumb things at the wrong time. Hank let the Hadleys know he meant business again by cocking the second hammer of his shotgun.

There was no turning back now, of that I was certain. I undid the thong on the hammer of my six-gun and lifted it out of the holster before letting it fall back in. I needed every edge I could get now. Behind me, I thought I heard Bob Wells snicker, and it made me mad.

"We come for the prisoner, Carston," George Hansom said.

"Those seem to be the only words you know how to speak the past few days, George," I said.

"Aw, to hell with it, Hansom," Carny Hadley said. "If you want something from this man, you're gonna have to take it." No sooner were the words out of his mouth than he was reaching for his six-gun, fully ready to kill me to back himself and his big words up.

One thing the Hadley brothers had in common with my boy Chance: they all liked and were good with guns. Carny Hadley was pulling his six-gun out and near pulling the trigger when I placed a slug high in his shoulder, knocking him back on his horse. He finally fell to the ground, dropping his gun as he did.

What scared me was the gunshot to my rear, for at first I wasn't sure who had fired it or if it was meant for me or what. Then I saw a red stain take form on Wilson Hadley's leg, right next to his holster. He dropped his pistol back into the holster and grabbed the gunshot wound, as though doing so would stop the bullet or lessen the pain. His hateful gaze fell on someone right in back of me, and when I looked up I saw Catherine Innes holding a shorter version of an old Colt Dragoon. A sheriff's model, I think Chance called it.

"Don't do it!" Hank then yelled out to the rest of the crowd, only this time he had the shotgun up and pressed hard against his shoulder. He meant business, and they all damn sure knew it. At least, if they didn't they were fools.

"Thank you, ma'am," I said, not feeling easy enough to look at the woman yet. These Hadleys could be tricky fellows when they wanted to be. And none of them liked losing. Hell, nobody does.

"My pleasure, Marshal." Somehow I just knew she was smiling when she said it. Something in her words sounded like that, if you know what I mean.

George Hansom's face was as white as if he'd seen a ghost, so I picked him to address about this whole matter. "George, you stop acting like some damn fool jackass and git the lot of you back to town and forget this foolishness about hanging a man."

"Yes, sir, Marshal." I was right. He was scared good enough. "You betcha. You can count on me. Come on, boys. Let the marshal do his job."

A couple of them gathered up the Hadleys and proceeded to get the hell out of there, just like I'd told them.

"And, George?"

"Yes, sir?"

"You bring any more of these Hadleys with you next time you try this foolishness and I'll kill them *and* you! Understand?"

His eyes got big and round, damn near falling out of his head. "Oh, yes, sir. It won't happen again, I assure you."

Then he and the rest were gone.

"Can we get going now?" Blacksnake Hank growled, back in his less than sociable mood, which was mad at the world when he was late.

"Anything you say, driver," I said with a grin and got into the coach.

I was about to sit down when I got a glimpse of Bob Wells. He was wearing a sneer on his face and I didn't like it, for I supposed it to be the one he had on him when I heard him snicker at me a few minutes before. Crouched down, I had one hand against the back of the coach for support. It was all I needed. I swung my right at Wells and hit him hard on the jaw. His head snapped back and bounced off the back of the coach, and for a second there he was unconscious.

Then I took my seat, acting as though nothing had happened.

Wells was bleeding from the lip, and the anger had quickly arisen in him, but his hands were tied behind his back and his feet were shackled with leg irons, so I knew he wasn't going to make a move. Not now, anyway.

"What did you hit me for?" he asked angrily.

"Yes, Marshal, why did you hit him?" Catherine Innes said, wanting to know the same thing.

I gave Wells a hard look and said, "Because you talk too much. Now, shut up!"

All I could hear was Blacksnake Hank cussing his six-horse hitch.

CHAPTER

★ 7 ★

That was some pretty handy shooting you done back there, ma'am," I said about an hour later. I'd reached a point where I had to say something. The three of us had sat through an hour's worth of time with nothing more than Blacksnake Hank's cussing and the movements of the stagecoach to entertain us, and I don't mind telling you I was getting mighty tired of both. The woman, Catherine Innes, was either infatuated with the scenery as we passed it or was well disciplined and had willed herself to silence. Bob Wells, he knew better than to utter a sound and had shrunk back into the corner on the left side of me, minding his own business.

"I had a good teacher," she replied with a knowing

smile. "Papa always said a woman had to keep her wits about her in a land like this."

"Your daddy was a wise man." Likely a good shot, too, I thought to myself, although I didn't say it. Nor did I press the issue. "Want to thank you again, ma'am, for your assistance," I added. "I'd likely have collected some lead my own self ary you hadn't handled that six-gun the way you did."

"I'm glad I could help." For a minute she looked as though she would turn back toward the window and the scenery, but what she did was glance out the window only briefly before turning her attention back to me. I hoped I wasn't staring at her that hard. Margaret Ferris would likely shoot me if she saw me doing that. Miss Innes stuck out a dainty, well-manicured hand and smiled at me. "Please, Marshal, call me Catherine if you like," she said in what I thought to be a soft, easy tone.

I shook the offered hand, making sure I put forth an extra effort not to give her my manliest grip lest I break her hand and what I was sure were some of the tiniest bones I'd ever seen on a woman.

"I'm Will . . . Will Carston," I said by way of introduction. I reckon my smile was a mite late. Maybe because I was still looking over her features the way I was. Not that I was admiring her beauty, you understand, although she had a good deal of it, I'll admit. Mostly, I'd gotten in the habit over the years of trying to match up faces with the ones I'd seen on the wanted posters I got every once in a while. Part of a lawman's habit, I reckon. Nothing romantic about it, not a-tall.

"I'm glad to meet you, Will."

"Same here, ma'am . . . I mean Miss Catherine." I

gave Bob Wells a critical glance out of the corner of my eye before saying, "Too bad it had to be under these circumstances."

"One does what one must," she said and let it go at that. I reckon that was her way of resolving a rather ugly situation, being in the presence of an outlaw and a killer and all.

"Yes, ma'am."

The conversation sort of dried up as fast as the desertlike land we were traveling through and stayed that way the rest of the afternoon. Not that you could blame anyone. Hell, once you got past palavering about the lack of rain in the area and all that sand it wasn't falling on, why, you'd pretty much exhausted your subject matter for stagecoach-riding conversation. As far as asking questions, well, you just didn't. After you'd been in this land long enough, you came to understand that asking what wasn't none of your business in the first place was likely to get you killed. Best thing a man could do was mind his own business and wait for the fellow across from him to voluntarily open up about who he was and where he'd come from and where he was going. It was a whole lot safer.

We pulled into the relay station about an hour before sundown, which was just fine with me. Supposedly there was a meal waiting for us inside the log cabin, and I thought I spotted an outhouse in back of the cabin. I'd been on stagecoaches before and knew that although the bottom portion of your body tends to go numb on you when you're riding those long stretches, why, once you get out and start moving about, it's amazing what bodily functions you're reminded you have to take care of. If you get my drift.

A husband and wife ran the station, and Catherine

took to gabbing with the woman as Hank and the husband unhitched the teams and led them away to the corral. While they were hitching the fresh team up, Wells and me made use of the outhouse and moved inside the cabin in hopes of finding food available.

Thank God there was.

Catherine and Wells and me were making our way through some roast beef, gravy, and biscuits by the time Blacksnake Hank sat down at the community table. And coffee, don't forget the black stuff. Got to have that to keep you going out here. Yes, sir.

"You're an awfully quiet man, sir," Catherine said to Hank as she dabbed a napkin at her lips when she was finished.

I reckon no one had told her that when you sit down to home cooking out here, why, you can forget your war stories until the food has been eaten. Keeping your belly full can be a right irregular thing to do out here sometimes.

"Don't let him fool you, Miss Catherine," I said, sopping up the last of the gravy on my plate with a spare biscuit. The biscuits were nothing like Sarah Ann or the Ferris women would make, but they were passable for traveling food. "Old Hank's got near as many stories to tell as I have."

"True," Hank said, nodding through a mouthful of meat. "True."

"I imagine they're quite exciting," Catherine said, as though urging Hank to tell a story right now. I knew better than that, for, skinny as he was, why, Hank could eat a horse if he had a mind to. It was another five minutes of stuffing his mouth, sopping up gravy and chewing between gulps of coffee before Blacksnake Hank had anything to say.

"Mostly, ma'am, the experiences I've had are awfully dull," he said with a straight face. "Cain't compare worth a whit with them dime novels I hear they got out now."

"Really?" Catherine said in pure rejection, although I had a notion it was playacting that she was doing. "I was so hoping this land would have some interesting stories I could pass on to my students. I'm studying to be a teacher, you know."

Hank pulled his pocket watch out, spied it with one cocked eye, replaced it, drank the second half of his coffee down in one swallow, and silently pointed to the cup until the woman of the house refilled it for him.

"Well, there was that Methodist minister I was carrying oncet," he said when he got his voice back.

"Really?" Catherine was taking a sudden interest in our driver and his story.

"Yes, ma'am. Come to a bad ford, we did. The stream was swollen by rains and had commenced to move back, making the banks awful slippery. Mind you, now, ma'am, I've been in many a sittyation like this afore. Many a one. Only one way to get across, you see. But like I say, I had this religious man on board my stagecoach."

"Really?" Catherine asked again, puzzled. "What would that have to do with getting across a swollen stream?"

Hank looked at me and said, "She ain't been on too many coach rides, has she?"

"I reckon not," I replied with a shrug.

"I yells out 'Preacher! I want you to get out and walk across that ford.' Lots of these holier-than-thou types act like they can walk on water, you know. But the preacher, why, he's looking as dumbfounded as you are, ma'am.

"He says, 'Why?'"

"So I tells him how old Ben Holladay has told all us drivers not to cuss the hosses, but I can't cross the damned ford unless I do. It's the only way them dunderheaded animals will understand a human sometimes."

"Really? What happened?" Catherine asked.

"Why, that old minister give me his permission to cuss away as long as we'd get the coach across that ford," Hank said.

"I see," Catherine said, looking disappointed. "Is there something significant about that story?" she added as she struggled to get to her feet.

Hank was taken aback that the woman had the gall to ask such a question. "Why, ma'am, I do believe that's about the only time I ever heard a man of the cloth make taking the Maker's name in vain to be fine and dandy!"

Catherine Innes had a pleasant smile on her face only a few seconds later when the husband who ran the relay station stuck his head inside the cabin.

"Team's hooked up and raring to go, Hank," he said.

Hank took another quick gander at his pocket watch and nodded. "Reckon it's that time." To the passengers, he announced, "Time to git, folks."

So we did.

CHAPTER

★ 8 ★

I reckon we stopped for fresh horses at least once during the night, but I don't recall just where it was. Blacksnake Hank had the good sense not to wake any of us from what little sleep we were able to get. Hell, even riding on a bouncy stagecoach won't bother a man that much when it comes to sleeping out of pure exhaustion. I reckon that was what got me through the night.

Of course, I'd made sure Bob Wells wasn't going to try anything funny while I was getting my beauty rest. Hank lent me some extra rope he carried in the rear boot of the coach, and I secured my prisoner to the side of the coach he was seated near. In fact, he was all but bound and gagged in that one position, if you'd like to consider it that. At first he started to object, but

55

all I had to do was give him a hard look and ball up my fist one time and he shut his mouth and took it like a man. Got to know how dentists must feel while doing their work, I did.

The sun was on the rise when the stagecoach jolted me awake as we pulled into another relay station. The normal world was coming awake, so I reckoned it was time for us to do the same. I managed to catch a glimpse of Catherine as she leaned against a self-fashioned pillow, still fast asleep. She looked almighty pretty lying there like that, a mite like my Cora did in the mornings I was up before her. I reckon there is something peaceful about the early time of day that gives a body hope to carry on the rest of the time Old Sol is up. I don't know about you, hoss, but I can remember days when it sure did help to have that kind of hope when first light come along. Yes, sir.

"Relay station!" I heard Hank yell at the top of his lungs as he pulled back on the reins and we swung into a well-worn path before another cabin of sorts. His words brought life into Bob Wells and Catherine Innes.

Inside we took another meal while Hank and one of the relay men changed the six-horse hitch. Instead of a husband and wife, it was two men who worked this station. The one inside wasn't a half-bad cook, either. The slabs of meat he put on our plates could have been boiled beef that was seeing its second serving on a plate, from the looks of it. But if you add enough salt you can give taste to just about anything. Which is what I did. At least he kept from burning the hell out of the scrambled eggs. I reckon the coffee and biscuits were what he had going for him, although neither was as good as I remember Cora or Margaret Ferris making. But like I said, there's times you can't be choosy about what you eat, and this was one of them. You find out right quick that on a stagecoach trip time is of the essence. Especially to men like Blacksnake Hank.

"I'm surprised you didn't get any sleep," Catherine said to Hank when he plunked his get-up end down at the community table.

"Well, ma'am, the company don't pay me for sleeping," he said as he cut up his meat. Apparently Hank didn't care what it looked like or how it might taste as long as it was dead and on his plate. Then, in a lower, secretive voice, he said, "But I'll tell you a secret if you keep it to yourself."

"You can trust me," Catherine said back in the same secretive way.

Hank, upon hearing her words, gave me a glance and a grin, both of us knowing that it wasn't in a woman to keep her mouth shut about much, not in our experience, I was sure. I returned the smile, making sure the woman didn't see me.

"I manage to get me an hour or two's worth of sleep at night when I'm driving these teams," Hank said with a nod. "Yes, I do."

"But how?" Catherine asked with a frown.

"It's these horses, ma'am."

"What about them?"

"Why, they know these trails better than I do!"

The look on Hank's face was dead serious, but his words had gotten Catherine Innes to laughing.

"I see," she said after a minute or so of laughter.

"Oh, it may seem funny, ma'am, but I'm dead serious," Hank continued, still wearing a grave look on his mug.

"Why?"

"Don't you realize what would happen, ma'am, if word of what those horses know about these trails got back to the company headquarters?" Hank said, all business. "Why, one of them horses would have my job!"

I'd heard Hank tell new passengers his tale before, and it was always fun seeing them react to it. Catherine Innes, well, she had a sense of humor, I'll give her that. Gave out a good laugh as Hank dug into his grub.

"You're right, Will," she said as we reboarded the coach and Hank climbed up on his seat. "He does have an awful lot of stories."

"Yes, ma'am," I said in agreement. "Almost as many as me."

I ain't been outdone as a storyteller since the last time I seen Old Gabe. For all you young Dan'l Boones, that's Jim Bridger, one of the best of the mountain men. And likely the best damned liar I ever did come across in my life.

I don't know if it was because we were heading north or because the season was coming to an end, but it wasn't all that hot that second day. Hell, maybe it was a combination of both. Something told me I should have known what the weather would be like, but I couldn't recall doing that much traveling up in the mountains, not after the frost set in, anyway. I'd spent my youth as a mountain man back in the 1830s, then signed up with the Texas Rangers just before the Mexican War. The farthest I could ever recall traveling to catch some desperadoes as a Ranger was a couple of hundred miles. But this trip would be close to a thousand miles by the time I was through, so maybe there would be a significant change in the weather by the time I reached Fort Dodge. After all, this was the right time of the year for a change to take place, the very end of the fall season.

We'd only been on the trail a couple of hours that morning when I heard Hank cussing to himself and pulling his teams to a halt.

"Another relay station this soon?" Catherine asked curiously.

"I don't think so," I replied as I drew my gun and stuck my head out the window. "What's the holdup, Hank?"

"If it's a holdup, he's either got a lot of sand or he's crazy," Hank said, sounding more nasty than fearful.

I heard him cocking the hammers on that shotgun of his, so I climbed down from the coach, my Remington firmly in hand, as I admonished Catherine from doing anything foolish, like getting off the coach.

A lone rider came at us from the far side. I was about to ask Hank why he didn't try to outrun him, when I recalled what he'd told me once before in a similar circumstance. "Seen too many a good horse of mine take lead from these types," he'd said. "Besides, I'm just as willing to die as the horses are. Part of what I get paid for, you know." So I kept my mouth shut for the moment and let the driver handle the situation. After all, it was his coach.

"If you're looking for gold, I ain't carrying any this trip," he said in a firm way, ready to let fly a load from his shotgun at even the hint of a sudden wrong move. "And if you're looking for mail, why, I doubt you could read it anyway."

"The only thing I want is a passenger of yours," the rider said as he came to a halt, kicking up a swirl of dust about him as he reined in his mount. "I need to speak to Will Carston."

"You sure do got a following, Marshal," Hank said, slowly letting the hammers of the shotgun down. "I hope this ain't gonna happen often. I still got a schedule to make."

I thought I'd recognized the voice, and when the dust cleared I knew I'd been right. But I was just as surprised as Hank had been.

"Pardee? Pardee Taylor?" I said in disbelief. "Is that you?"

"You bet, Marshal," he said.

"What in the hell are you doing out here?" I asked, still not sure I could believe my eyes.

Pardee seemed embarrassed in a way. "I hope you didn't figure I come following you like some puppy dog, Marshal, because I didn't."

I didn't say it, but that was *exactly* what I was thinking. Yes, sir. Pardee had been trying to impress me ever since he'd decided to stay sober some time back. He was somewhere in between Wash and Chance as far as age went, but I swear sometimes the man acted like a little child. Yes, that was exactly what I was thinking.

"It was Chance sent me, Marshal," he said, a good deal of pride showing as he spoke. "Said he needed a good man for something as important as this, so he sent me." Sure, Chance, I thought to myself. My older son, the one I'd left behind as the acting marshal in my absence, had sent Pardee just to get him out of his hair.

"Well, what is it, man? You've got a message to deliver or what?" I asked.

"It's this, Marshal," Pardee said and dug a fist into

the inside pocket of his jacket. Then, dismounting, he walked over and handed me a set of papers that looked awful familiar. "It's the extradition papers. Chance said you had to have 'em to get your prisoner transferred to the proper authorities, so he sent me to catch up with you and give 'em to you."

I glanced over them and sure enough, that's what they were. Then I searched the inside pocket of my own coat and discovered that I had indeed forgotten the damn things! And Chance was right, I would need them when the time came.

"Well, I thank you, Pardee, I surely do," I said and stuck out my hand in thanks. "I'm glad you could catch up with me." I walked over to his horse, which was breathing hard and aching to blow, I was guessing. I undid the cinch strap and let him do just that. "Looks like you rode mighty hard to get here, too."

"If you two are through palavering, I've still got a schedule to keep," an irritated Hank said as he pulled out his pocket watch and gave it a gander.

"Yes, we're through, Hank," I said.

"No, we ain't," Pardee cut in, sounding like he didn't really care what kind of a hurry the driver was in.

"I hope you ain't a slow thinker, son," Hank said with a growl, "'cause you got exactly two minutes to get whatever's on your mind said and out and be shut of it. Now, just start flapping your jaws. . . . You've wasted a good ten seconds already."

"Marshal, you need another guard, and I'm your man," Pardee said, speaking as fast as I'd ever heard him talk. "Besides, you seen yourself my horse is dead tired. I don't think he could be ridden much farther without collapsing, not with me on him anyway."

61

All he had to do was let that first sentence out and I knew what he was getting at. But I kept seeing Pardee dancing around the way he did when Wells and his gang had held up the bank in Twin Rifles. If he'd gotten out of the way, why, I'd have been able to stop more of the gang than I had. He was just clumsy sometimes, that's what Pardee was. And picturing him coming along as a guard was almost a laughable thought. Hell, with my luck, he'd wind up handing his six-gun over to Wells for safekeeping while he went off into the bushes to do his business. Still, I didn't know what to say, didn't know how to say anything without hurting the man's feelings.

Hank settled that for me.

"Got any money for fare?" he asked Pardee.

"No." Pardee shrugged. This was a detail he apparently hadn't thought about.

"Well, that settles that," I said, hoping this conversation was over now.

"But—"

"Can you handle that six-gun at your side?" Hank asked. "And that rifle in your saddle boot?"

Pardee smiled like a youngster looking at his presents on Christmas morning. "You bet, mister."

And he could, that much I knew. I couldn't forget the look on his face when he'd thrown down on Bob Wells as the gang leader tried to escape. "Intense" was the word that came to mind. He would have killed the man if circumstances had called for it, and done it without a blink of the eye. Oh, yes, Pardee Taylor could use his guns all right.

"All right, here's how it's gonna be," Hank said, making a final decision. "I ain't left a man out in the middle of Comanche country alone yet. So if the marshal can't use you for a deputy or a guard or whatever, I'm hiring you temporary for the stage-coach company."

"Really?" Pardee was genuinely surprised.

"Pull your rifle out of the boot and keep it with you the rest of this trip, son. If there's room, you can sit inside. If not, plant your git-up end up here next to me."

"I really appreciate this, sir, I really do," Pardee said, still reminding me of a young boy rather than the full-grown man he was.

"Don't call me *sir,* damn it!" Hank growled, as though he detested the word. "I *work* for a living! It's Hank. You call me *Hank.*"

"Yes, sir," Pardee said in a pleased tone, then tied his mount to the rear of the stagecoach, grabbed his rifle, and headed for the seat Hank had offered him atop the coach.

"There's only one thing you've got to remember when you sit up here, son," I heard Hank grumble as Pardee climbed up next to him.

"What's that?"

"I don't care how goddamn grateful you are, son. *Just keep your mouth shut!*"

It was the morning of the third day that I exchanged my Sunday-go-to-meeting jacket for my good old buckskin jacket. I'd also discarded my new white shirt and string tie for a regular blue work shirt and a worn cowhide vest I usually sported back in town.

"Not too formal this morning, are you, Will?" Catherine Innes commented to me with a smile as we boarded the stagecoach yet again.

"That's a fact, Miss Catherine. It surely is a fact," I said. I tried to return the smile, for the two of us had begun to get along right well these past couple of days. The first-name basis we were now on had come real easy to me, as I was sure it had to her. "The truth is," I added as we settled into our seats and Hank got to yelling at his six-horse hitch, "those fancy suits ain't much better for occasions other than leaving and arriving on a stagecoach. Besides, that suit was getting awful tight on me." Not to mention the fact that it was getting a whole lot cooler during the evenings and my buckskin jacket, even though it was large and roomy, tended to be a mite more on the warm side.

"No, I guess there isn't really anyone to impress out here, is there?" Catherine said with a smile.

I could tell that Bob Wells was wanting to say something smart-alecky in the worst way, but all it took was a harsh glance from me to banish those thoughts from that yahoo's mind. I was more than certain that Bob Wells still remembered me hitting him hard across the mouth the other day. Not that I'm bragging or anything, hoss. Hell, when you come right down to it there ain't no such a thing as bragging. You're either telling the truth or you're lying; it's that simple. And the truth of what damage I could do with my fists was all too evident to Bob Wells. Yes, sir.

Pardee Taylor was caught up in his role as a guard and spent most of his time up top with Hank. At one time he thought he'd spotted some Comanch', but it was a false alarm. Not that I wasn't expecting to be hit by renegade Indians, if it wasn't someone who was mad at me for keeping the likes of Bob Wells alive. But if they did show up, I was figuring it would be real interesting to see how Pardee Taylor, Twin Rifles' one time drunk and bully, would stand up to them. Real interesting.

Catherine Innes and me spent most of the morning getting out one or two more stories about our background to each other. By noon it had heated up a good deal and we both found our throats going dry on us, so we gave up storytelling for the quieter things that can be done on a stagecoach trip. Which isn't much. For Catherine it was going back to looking at the scenery as we made our way farther north with each mile. For me it was the choice of taking a nap—which I reluctantly turned down once I remembered that I had Bob Wells sitting not that far from me—or looking out the window at surroundings I could view in a hundred different places in Texas and never know I'd missed anything. After all, sagebrush is sagebrush, whether it's sitting still or rolling along with the wind. However, I will confess that at one point I almost asked Pardee Taylor to sit inside the coach and palaver with me. Then I remembered Pardee's depth when it came to conversations and realized that I'd likely have a more stimulating talk with one of Hank's six-horse hitch. If you get my drift.

About midafternoon we made another relay station stop, and I got out to find the outhouse while Pardee helped Hank and the station manager change horses. I toted Bob Wells with me, then plunked him down at the table inside the relay station. At least there was coffee to be had, which helped my throat some, considering the parched feeling I had in it.

What happened next scared me almost as much as I believe it did Catherine and my prisoner.

He came through the door to the relay station. Maybe *busted* through the door would be more accurate. In one hand he held a half-empty bottle and in the other was a six-gun he was waving in the air. He let out a yell like I hadn't heard since Wash demonstrated what he called his "rebel yell." Catherine Innes let out a scream before covering her mouth with a shaking hand.

"Are you crazy, mister?" Bob Wells asked. Apparently he didn't like that pistola waving around any more than I did.

"Aw, shut up!" the stranger said in a slurred voice, the way most drunks will talk.

"Whoa, now, old hoss," I said, getting up from the table I was having my coffee at. "You want to just hold it down some, what with the lady present and all. This ain't a saloon, you know."

The crazed eyes of the drunk focused on me now as he squinted like a man just coming in after a day's work in the sun. For a second the squint turned into a frown and he cocked his head sideways.

"And why would I do that, mister?"

Now, hoss, I've been a lawman for a number of years. Fact of the matter is I've stayed a lawman for that number of years by playing each incident I got caught up in with a different approach. Nothing like my son, Chance, who'll go charging into hell with a bucket of water, with nothing more in mind than the pure intent of putting out the fire and skating on the ice. That ain't the sanest way of handling things, if you ask me. On the other hand, even with a whole passelful of holes in him, Chance is very much alive these days. But this drunk before me, why, he was posing a real challenge, especially when you consider the fact that he had his gun out and I didn't.

"Because I'm asking you to real nice, son," I said in my friendliest tone of voice.

It hit him unexpected, I reckon. He looked at me cockeyed, the way one of these sorts will when he's out looking for a fight and itching for it besides. Acting like a good neighbor, why, he's not expecting that at all.

"All right, since you asked me nice like and all," the

drunk replied. He twirled the six-gun around his finger, the way some young Dan'l Boone will do, trying to show off and all, and planted it in his holster. "But not this. You can't have this," he added, holding his half-empty bottle close to his chest.

"Wouldn't touch it," I said. "Got my own poison over there," I added, nodding toward my cup of the black stuff.

"Say, do I know you from somewhere?" the stranger asked, giving me another cockeyed look, accompanied by a bewildered frown.

"No," I said, searching my memory real quick-like but coming up with nothing. "I don't think so. Why? *Do* you know me?"

"I'd swear I do."

"No. Can't help you, son. You've got the wrong man this time." I tried saying it with the same good-neighbor voice I'd used just a minute ago, hoping he wouldn't get mad and want to go back to fighting.

He shrugged and took a long swallow from his bottle. "If you say so." His words sounded friendly enough.

I was about to go back to my coffee, wondering if I could get another cup in before we had to leave again. That was when Hank came through the door, brushing his hat against his dusty dungaree's. I reckon it looked like he was going for his gun, for the stranger, drunk as he was, had that six-gun out of that leather in a flash, pointing it straight at Hank. I thought I noticed a wildness to his look then, something that hadn't been there when he'd first come in. This boy was in a killing mood, that look said.

"Mighty fast with a gun, sonny," Hank said, cool

as a cucumber. "I just hope you don't make a habit of shooting men who ain't drawed on you." Hank plopped his hat on the back of his head and held both hands out to his sides to indicate they were both free of firearms.

For a second Hank's words and gestures confused the drunken gunman. I reckon what really threw the lad was seeing Pardee Taylor step inside the relay station and stand next to Hank.

Come to think of it, Pardee kind of surprised me, too.

"I've got a six-gun if you want to try drawing that gun again," he said in a hard, even voice. It was a tone I'd seldom if ever heard the man speak in. And he sounded like he meant it.

The drunk looked at Pardee as though he thought the man was crazy. Then, after a brief smile to himself, he twirled his six-gun just as he'd done for me, planted it back in his holster, and said, "As long as it's self-defense, why not?"

Now, hoss, as tough as old Pardee was sounding, why, he just wasn't any kind of match for the man facing him now, especially after the speed I'd seen him draw his pistol with. Hell, if Pardee Taylor was that good, why, he'd been holding back on it for some years now, and Pardee just wasn't that kind of a person. If he'd managed to do something good, he made sure you knew about it, whether you wanted to or not. And drawing a six-gun wasn't anything I'd ever heard Pardee brag about.

With that in mind, I eased back my chair, hoping it wouldn't make much of a racket. If it did, neither man noticed it. Two quick steps was all it took to put me right behind the drunken gunman, and by that time I had my Remington out and ready for use.

"Drawing that pistola of yours would be a real mistake, son," I said, slowly sticking the barrel of my own handgun in his ribs as I spoke. "Now, why don't you just leave the gun alone and stick with that bottle of yours? I'd appreciate it if you would."

He looked over his shoulder at me, once again giving me that cockeyed look, the same one he had not long ago. Then he smiled and said, "Sure. Why not? Lot of sense to what you're saying, friend. A lot of sense."

Then he sauntered over to a lone chair in the corner, took a seat in relative peace and quiet, and drank what was left in the bottle in one long swallow. He took a long glance at the bottle as he held it at arm's length. Then, as though he knew what was about to happen next, he slowly set the bottle on the floor and leaned his head back against the wall. His eyes closed, and I knew good and well he was passed out.

The manager of the relay station had a cup of coffee on the counter for Hank. But before he handed it to him, I saw him tilt a bottle of his own homemade whiskey into the coffee. That would give it a livelier taste, if my recollection was right.

Hank drank about half of it in one swallow his own self, let out a long sigh of relief, and said, "Thanks, Henry, I appreciate it a good deal." Then, to the rest of us, he said, "Time to git, folks. I got a schedule to keep, you know." Then he disappeared from sight.

"My, that was a brave thing to do, Will," Catherine said as I made my way to the drunk and quietly lifted his six-gun from his holster.

"Don't give this back to him until you've filled him with a pot of coffee," I said to Hank, the relay station manager.

"Sure thing, Marshal," was his reply.

"Sticking a gun in a man's back ain't too awful brave, ma'am," Pardee said in his somewhat less than humble way. "Facing the business end of a pistol, now, that's brave. Yes, ma'am."

But Catherine Innes wasn't all that impressed and simply walked past Pardee without even bothering to comment on his remarks.

"Well, what do you think, Will?" Pardee said. I had a strong notion he was looking for my approval.

"I think he'd have killed you ary you'd have gone through with that damn stupid shooting," I said angrily. "I think you been listening to too many of those outlandish stories Chance spins these days."

That hit him where it hurt, where it hurts with every man. A body's got to have a certain amount of pride, you know.

"But Chance said—"

"Pardee," I said with a frown, sticking a stubby finger into the man's chest. "Let me make you aware of something right here and now. Chance is Chance, and Pardee Taylor is Pardee Taylor, and the difference between the two is considerable."

I stormed out of the relay station and got on the stagecoach. Pardee was quick to follow, climbing up on the box alongside Hank, whether the driver wanted him there or not.

But as Hank cussed his six-horse hitch and we left the relay station, it wasn't Pardee Taylor's pride that was on my mind. Mostly, I was wondering how in the devil that drunk we'd just left behind could have mistaken me for someone he knew. I couldn't recall seeing him anyplace that I'd ever been. So who was he?

More important was the realization that whoever he was, drunk or sober, I'd bet he was a dangerous man.

CHAPTER
★ 10 ★

"Say, Rachel, what's wrong with your mother?" Dallas
Bodeen asked as he pushed aside the empty plate. Will
Carston had recommended the food Margaret and
Rachel Ferris put out on a daily basis once the former
Texas Ranger had decided to stay on in Twin Rifles a
while back. It wasn't hard for him to get in the habit of
using one of Margaret's prime biscuits to sop up any
gravy on his plate.

Like her mother, Rachel had gotten to know the
regular customers and their habits, so picking up the
empty plate was as natural for her as it was for Dallas
Bodeen to leave it purely empty.

"I don't know, Mr. Bodeen," she said in a worried
tone, as she refilled Dallas's cup and set the pot of
coffee down on the community table. "She made a big

to-do about that woman who was going on the stage-coach when the marshal boarded it. Acting like she's worried the woman will get her claws in the marshal and she'll lose Will and—" Suddenly Rachel's words stopped as she realized what she was saying, and her hand quickly covered her mouth, as though that would keep her from saying any more. The blush that crept up her neck didn't help the way she was feeling, either.

Dallas gave a sly grin as he took a sip of his coffee, formulating in his mind what needed to be said to this young lady. Hell, a man spent enough time in his life making a fool out of himself, why add to someone else's ill feeling? And Dallas Bodeen could tell a good many stories about the times he'd made a fool of himself. A good many.

"I'll let you in on a secret, Rachel," he said.

"Oh, go on" was Rachel's reply. "Mama says you ain't nothing but an old storyteller."

"True," Dallas admitted, rubbing his jaw, as though in contemplation. "On the other hand, I've been known to tell the truth once in a while, too. And what I'm about to tell you is the truth."

Rachel eyed the old man suspiciously, not sure she could take him at his word. "Honest?"

"You betcha, darlin'."

"Well, all right." The younger Ferris woman looked about to see if anyone else was listening, discovered the room was empty of customers, and took a seat across from Dallas Bodeen.

"Now, woman, I've only been here a short time, compared to many another of the folks in this town, but I learned more than just reading sign when I was a Ranger. Yes, ma'am."

Rachel frowned. "What are you talking about?"

"Why, I learned to read *people,* I did!"

"So what's the secret?"

"Well, Rachel, it 'pears to me you're thinking it's only you who knows how your mama feels about old Will Carston," he said in what he considered a secretive tone.

"Oh?" This little piece of knowledge apparently did come as a surprise to Rachel. "Is that so?"

"That's a fact, ma'am. Why, I've heard a couple, three dozen different people gaggling their tongues about Will and Margaret," he said. "And that, ma'am, is no story."

"No," Rachel said, drawing the word out in disbelief.

"Oh, yes, ma'am." Hearing these words and the determination Dallas Bodeen used in speaking them brought a full blush to Rachel Ferris's face. She had come to know this old man in the few months he'd been in Twin Rifles, and she'd discovered that he was indeed a lot like Will Carston. So if Dallas said it was so, then it was so.

"Oh, I feel so . . ." Rachel started to say as she pulled out a handkerchief and dabbed at her eyes.

"Don't you worry about it none, Miss Rachel," Dallas said, placing a callused hand over her own. "I reckon it's just that some people outguess what others figure they got as a secret.

"As for Margaret thinking she's losing Will to another woman, why, that just ain't a-going to happen," he added with a wink and a nod.

"And how would you know that?"

"Why, Miss Rachel, the only woman who ever really got her claws into old Will was Cora, and she was the *only* woman Will was ever satisfied with." He paused a moment in thought before saying, "Unless, of course, Miss Margaret was to set her cap for Will. I got to tell you, honey, that is one purely determined woman, I'll give her that," he added with a chuckle.

"Really?" Rachel couldn't believe what she was hearing.

"Yes, ma'am. So you see, Miss Margaret ain't got nothing to worry about with that woman on the stagecoach. Why, Will Carston's got a better chance of getting shot at than being romanced by some woman on a stagecoach."

Rachel took both of Dallas's hands in her own and gave him a smile he hadn't seen on her in a few days. "Thanks, Dallas, thanks a lot." She leaned across the table and kissed the old man, scraggly beard and all before picking up his plate and now empty coffee cup. With a wider smile, she said, "You know, it's good to have a friend like you to talk to. Yes, Dallas, it sure is."

"Now you've got the idea," Dallas said, presenting a smile of his own. "Everything's gonna be just fine. Yes, ma'am, it's gonna be just fine."

"Yes, Dallas, I think it will," Rachel said, still smiling. Then she was gone.

It made Dallas Bodeen feel good to know he could cheer up a young lady like that. God only knew the youngsters trying to make a go of it on this frontier were going to need all the encouragement they could get. Back in the old days, why, things were a whole lot simpler. It just seemed that as the years went by, life got more and more difficult. Yes, sir, Rachel needed that kind of cheering up. In fact, Dallas was sure she could find a way to convince her mother that everything would be all right, too.

The only thing that troubled Dallas Bodeen as he left the Ferris House was the same gnawing feeling that Margaret Ferris had been experiencing. But it had nothing to do with a woman. Somewhere in his gut, in his instinct, Dallas Bodeen just *knew* that his best friend, Will Carston, was in some kind of trouble. Shooting trouble!

But at the moment there didn't seem to be a damn thing he could do about it!

CHAPTER
★ 11 ★

Staying alive can be a real chore in this land. I learned right early in life to trust a lot more than what I saw, namely that little voice in the back of my skull that told me things weren't right, weren't right at all. I don't mind telling you that ever since we'd left that relay station, I'd had that feeling about this trek to Fort Dodge.

It was the fourth day of our trip, and something wasn't right. Someone was trailing us, my little voice said. And what kept sticking in my mind most was the fact that the young lad who was drunk in that relay station, why, he might well be the one trailing me. I kept wondering where it was he knew me from, for I sure as blazes didn't know him, from Adam or anyone else.

"Something bothering you, Will?" Catherine asked, a note of worry in her voice.

"Yeah, Will, you do look almighty worried," Pardee Taylor said. I reckon that foolhardy incident Pardee had been involved in back at the relay station—and damn near got himself killed over, I might add—got him to feeling like a real man, for he'd suddenly taken to calling me Will rather than addressing me as the marshal of Twin Rifles. Mind you, a lot of folks in Twin Rifles called me by my given name, but I'd known most of them a goodly while, which accounted for the familiarity. Pardee, on the other hand, well, he might not *live* long enough to get friendly with if he kept on acting as reckless as he did at that relay station. Blacksnake Hank had apparently had enough of him, too, which accounted for him now sitting inside the coach with Catherine, Wells, and me.

"Age, Pardee. It's age," I said.

"Oh, come on, Will, you're not that old, are you?" Catherine said, trying to be kind, I reckon.

"Well, Miss Catherine, that's real kind of you," I replied. "But you see, it ain't me being as old as I am so much as it is what I've lived through to get this old. If you follow my train of thought."

"What he means, ma'am," Pardee said before anyone else could get a word in edgewise, "is he's been through a whole lot of adventures in his life. And smart as he is, why, Will's remembered near all of 'em, which makes him that much more ready for the next donnybrook that comes up."

"I see," Catherine said in a droll tone of voice.

"Honest, ma'am," I said, feeling a touch of red crawl up the back of my neck, "I didn't hire him to say it. Not a-tall."

"Does that mean I have to figure out what's truth and what's fiction all by myself?" she asked, that same amused look on her face.

"Let me put it this way, ma'am," I said, trying to explain myself. "I'll be the first one to admit that Pardee ain't much in the line of speechmaking, but most of what he's said is true. As for the rest, why, I reckon that'll give you something to challenge your mind until we hit the next relay station."

"All right," she said with a smile. Then, after a few minutes' pause, her tone turned serious. "But you are worried about something, aren't you?"

"Yes, ma'am. I reckon you'd both be right about that," I said and proceeded to tell them my thoughts about the drunken lad at the relay station and how I couldn't get him out of my mind. "Yes, ma'am, it's bothering me something powerful. That it is," I concluded.

"Well, I wouldn't worry," she said, apparently taking the whole thing lightheartedly. Looking at Pardee, who was seated next to her on the bench, she smiled in a playful way and added, "We can always have Mr. Taylor show his prowess as a fancy man with a gun again and save us all by himself."

"You're funning me, ma'am, ain't you?" Pardee said, looking a mite foolish at the moment.

"Yes, Mr. Taylor," Catherine said with a smile and patted Pardee's big hand as though she were talking to a baby brother. "I'm funning you, as you say. Please don't take it seriously."

"No, ma'am. I won't." Pardee gave off a sheepish smile of his own.

There was no telling where this conversation was

going to lead, but then, I never did get a chance to find out.

"Visitors, Marshal!" Hank yelled out from his box above us. "Don't look none too friendly neither!"

Comanch' was the first thing that entered my mind. Although they had no use for mail or gold, the Comanches didn't care for the white man riding through their territory one little bit. So occasionally they would send out a war party to put the fear of God into the stage driver and his passengers.

But it wasn't Comanches at all. When I pulled my Remington and looked out the window, I saw about a half dozen men, maybe more, riding our way. They'd been riding fast enough so they'd gained on the coach quite quickly between the time Hank announced their arrival and the time I got a glance in their direction. From their garb, I gauged them to be white men, likely bandits of some sort. It was when they got a mite closer that I thought I recognized them.

It was the Wells Gang!

Hank was holding to his steadfast rule and pulling his coach to a halt, getting ready to make a stand.

"What's he doing?" Catherine yelled in a voice filled with fear.

"He must have had relatives at the Alamo, ma'am?" I said as I fired a shot at the gang, which was nearly on us now.

"The what?"

"We get out of this scrape, I'll explain it to you, ma'am," I said to her. "Right now you get that pretty head of yours down and out of sight."

Hank's rifle went off, and one of the gang members dropped from the saddle, although I wasn't sure he was dead. At the moment I didn't really care, either. Hell, the son of a bitch was out of this game, and that was good enough for me.

I made the mistake of firing at one of them while the coach was still jostling me about, missing him by a goodly piece. Then I heard a grunt behind me, turned, and saw Bob Wells kicking Pardee Taylor in the side as Pardee was taking up a defense position on the opposite side of the coach from me. It was then I remembered I'd been so mad at Pardee for the reckless stunt he'd pulled that I hadn't even bothered to tie my prisoner to the side of the coach, as I'd done so far this trip. So much for letting emotions get the best of you.

I had to turn near full around to do it, but I laid the barrel of my Remington up alongside Bob Wells's head and made sure I saw him sink to the floor before I turned back to the window I'd been firing out of. Pardee, I noticed, had a hand on his side and was groaning in pain. Not that I could blame him, for I'd had the experience my own self a number of years back, and I don't mind telling you it hurt like hell.

Out of the corner of my eye I saw Catherine, hunched down like I'd told her, but digging inside the pockets of her skirts for that pistol she'd brandished a few days back when I'd had my run-in with the angry citizens of Twin Rifles.

I tossed another shot at the outlaws, who were getting closer and circling the coach now, almost like a warring party of renegade Indians would attack. I missed again and thought I knew what Chance meant when he talked about getting a bigger six-gun because he couldn't hit a damn thing. Chance was a damn good shot. In fact, I was a good shot, too, but I didn't seem to be able to hit anything right now.

I saw Catherine stick that Navy Colt she carried out the window in front of her and fire once, although she looked awful damn scared.

Then three horsemen rode quickly past me, all three firing at once, it seemed, as their bullets pierced the stagecoach. In fact, all I could hear was gunfire.

Which was also when the world came to an end for me and all I could see was pitch black as I fell forward.

CHAPTER

★ 12 ★

I was bouncing around in total darkness, swimming in a world where everyone but me could speak. There were words, strange ones from people I didn't know. Then I heard her words, the soft ones I knew would heal me. Cora was the only one who could bandage me up right. I'd been in more than one scrape after setting up our place in Twin Rifles, and Cora, my one and only love, had patched me up as well as any town doctor could have done. But now she was arguing with some strangers, men I didn't know, men I was afraid would hurt her. I tried to tell her to hush up, to be quiet. I tried to warn her, but the words wouldn't come out, and she kept arguing with them, kept trying to protect me. I loved that woman, but she was no use to anyone if she was dead. Finally I gave up trying, knowing it was no use, and slept. Yet in the background I heard the voices, angry voices, and even as I was jostled around in that blackness, I could hear them.

"There you go, Will." It was her voice—Cora's, I could have sworn—making me feel easy as she patched up my wound. I could count on her. I just knew I could. I tried focusing my eyes around the wet cloth she was applying to my face, to my forehead, and couldn't make out who she was. "Careful now. You got your head grazed by a nasty bullet."

"Who—" I started to say.

"I'm afraid I'm not Cora." The words came from Catherine Innes, and once I recognized her I thought I knew where I was and what I was supposed to be doing. The stagecoach. Bob Wells. Pardee Taylor. My hand went down to my side out of reflex, but my Remington was gone, as was my holster and gun belt. "I'm surprised you made it this far," she said, once again applying the damp cloth to my forehead.

"So am I" was all I could think to say. "Where are we? What happened to the others?"

Catherine Innes wrang the cloth out in a pan filled with water next to my bed, or wherever the hell I was lying. It sure wasn't the bed I rented at the Ferris House, I was certain of that much. I squinted past her and thought I saw some mean-looking yahoos standing across the room. I saw a window, through which light streamed, and knew I was in a shelter of some sort.

"Those men are members of the Wells Gang, or so I've been told," Catherine said, glancing cautiously over her shoulder, as though expecting to be hit for the words she spoke. If those varmints were as ugly and mean as they looked, she had a lot to worry about. "We're in a line shack of some sort, or maybe somebody's old cabin. I can't tell for sure."

"If you know what's good for you, you'll shut up, lady," one of the plug-uglies said with a growl. Catherine pursed her lips, not sure, by the look of her, whether she should say anything back to this yahoo for fear of reprisal of some sort. She needn't have worried.

The room was suddenly full of other people.

"You're the one oughta be shutting up, sonny." The voice came from the other side of me, or the other side of the room, take your pick. It was gravelly enough to belong to Blacksnake Hank. Once I managed to turn my addled head, I could readily see that it was Hank all right, sitting in a chair, his arm done up in a sling of some type. "You don't never talk to a lady like that, you sorry son of a—"

"Better shut your mouth, old man." Another voice I recognized. I didn't have to look to know it belonged to Bob Wells. Hell, it had that smart-alecky tone to it, so how could it be anyone else? "I can kill you any time I want to, you know."

Hank must have believed him, for he was surprisingly quiet now.

"What about Pardee?" I asked Catherine.

"He's on the floor over against the wall," she said in a sad way. "Mr. Wells kicked him pretty hard, I'm afraid. And when this gang of men took over the stagecoach, they did some more beating on him. From what I've seen, he may have some broken bones in his chest. I'm sure they're bruised at least."

I didn't feel any pain in my own chest, only the ringing sensation in my head. The rest of me felt reasonably well, too. The pain made me wonder if my head could get any bigger before it busted loose like a watermelon.

"What about me?" I asked when Wells had gone from the room and all that remained was the two plug-uglies, one in each corner of the room to my left. "I don't feel like I've been beat on as much as Pardee."

Catherine Innes blushed some. "In a way I guess you could say that you owe your life to me," she said in a soft voice, almost a whisper. "I don't know what made me do it, but I threw my arms around you when these madmen showed up and begged them not to harm you any more." A hint of a smile came to her face as she said, "I told them you were my fiancé."

"Now, why would you do something like that?" I asked out loud.

Catherine simply shrugged, obviously embarrassed to admit what she was about to say. "I guess I got to liking you, if you want to know the truth."

Talk about feeling uncomfortable! "Pardon me, ma'am, but that bullet must have done more damage to my head than I realized," I said. "I thought I just heard you say . . ."

Now that the words were out she must not have felt so uneasy about the whole situation. Or maybe it was seeing that I was the one who was a mite troubled about her words that made her rest easy.

"That's exactly what you heard," she said, now smiling the way a woman will when she knows she has the upper hand. And having the upper hand, why, that was when she leaned down and kissed me like she really meant it. "Gotta keep up the pretense," she said, then kissed me again. This time I kind of enjoyed it. In fact, the only thing that made me not enjoy it was the very real knowledge that Margaret Ferris would shoot me dead if she ever found out about this.

"Ain't you the lucky one," Hank said from across the room.

"Isn't that what engaged couples are supposed to do?" Catherine said with all the coyness of a saloon woman in the red-light district.

"In private, ma'am, in private," Hank whispered. You'd think he was some kind of minister worried about keeping all the commandments in their right order. Not that there was anything wrong in what he said. Hell, you didn't hold a woman's hand or kiss her in public unless you wanted everyone's lips a-flapping about when you were going to marry her. It was just the way things were.

"Don't make no never mind," one of the guards said with a chuckle. "The odds of you folks living another day or two are next to nothing."

What he meant by that, I had no idea. Were we going to be killed? Probably. But why hadn't they done us in at the site of the stagecoach? And just where the hell were we in proximity to the stagecoach? What had happened to it? Why bring the four of us along if all they were after was Bob Wells? My mind was too foggy to answer any of these questions, much less go into the whys and wherefores of them.

I only knew one thing for sure: like it or not, the Wells Gang had us as hostages and prisoners, one and the same.

CHAPTER
★ 13 ★

I don't know how she'd managed to do it, but
Catherine had tied a strip of cloth around my head
where the bullet had creased my skull. She seemed to
be making an awful fuss over me that day, especially
after that kiss she'd given me. I reckon she was indeed
taking a liking to me. Either that or she was putting on
a real good show for the gunmen holding us in that
line shack.

"Makes you look like one of them Barbary pirates,
it does," Hank said later in the day. At least he hadn't
lost his sense of humor. "You just ain't got the eye
patch, Marshal." That gave him something else to
laugh at. But then, he was the fellow with the broken
arm, not me, so if the laughter helped him get by, why,
more power to him.

"Well, I don't care how silly it looks, Will, you leave that bandage right where it is," Catherine said in an authoritative voice when I started to feel around the area of the wound.

At the risk of hearing more rasping smart-alecky remarks from Hank—likely something to the effect that my brains would dribble out of my head if I undid the bandage—I left the cloth where it was and held my curiosity in check for a while. At the moment I had more important things to tend to. Like figuring a way out of this mess.

Pardee Taylor regained consciousness later that day and got all sorts of apologetic about failing me as a guard.

"Don't worry about it, hoss," I said, trying to ease the humiliation he seemed to be feeling. Pointing to the bandage around my head, I added, "I wasn't doing so well my own self."

He also confirmed what Catherine had said about him being beaten even more after Wells kicked his side in. The way he was groaning told me he must have hurt like hell. And he could barely move around on the floor, which said more than any words he might have mumbled. I knew, because I'd been in some tough situations like that before, too.

Whoever did the cooking didn't know spit about making a decent meal, for we wound up eating something that resembled gruel, both in looks and in taste. Still, my stomach had been growling for a while, so I kept my thoughts to myself and made what I could of the meal.

Catherine made a grim face at her first taste of the supposed supper. "If this stuff or those guards don't kill us tonight, I'll volunteer to make breakfast for the

lot of us tomorrow morning," she said in all serious-
ness.

"I'm for that, missy," Hank said. "Ain't had food as
bad as this since my first wife tried cooking."

"I won't ask how long the marriage lasted," Pardee
said. Apparently he, too, was developing a sense of
humor.

"You're a wise man not to travel down that canyon,
son" was Hank's reply. He then went back to eating
the bland meal he'd been served.

By sundown I was feeling a mite better in the head,
neck, and shoulder region of my body, which was the
only part of me that hurt bad. The watermelon had
shrunk in size some. I was about to fade off to sleep
when Catherine approached me and made more fuss
about checking my head wound.

"Just look straight ahead," she commanded as one
of the guards held a lantern up for her to examine the
wound. Hank had stretched out on the floor beside
Pardee, and they'd both drifted off to sleep. "I almost
forgot about that wound of yours," Catherine said
when she saw the confusion on my face.

"Yes, ma'am," I said and let her go about her
business, although it did smart some when she put
fresh medicine on that wound before rebandaging it.

Surprisingly the wound didn't stop me from getting
a good night's sleep. I'd no sooner closed my eyes than
it seemed as though the sun was on the rise again. Of
course, when I looked around, I saw that a new set of
guards had replaced the old ones and was reminded
that we were still prisoners.

Catherine took over the cooking chores and did a
fine job of making at least a presentable meal for all of
us, considering what she had to work with. The meat

wasn't the tenderest I'd ever had, but she had made some gravy out of the grease and some biscuits to go along with it to make up for any shortcoming like a tough piece of meat. I reckon if it keeps the belly from growling it does the job. A cup of the black stuff always helps, too.

We were located in the back room of this line shack, or whatever it was, and when the day began to heat up, the guards opened both the window and the door to the front room to let a slight breeze circulate some fresh air among us. I carefully tried to stand up about noon, making sure I had the guard's permission just so he wouldn't shoot me for sport. That was when we were all hit by a surprise.

He came through the door of the line shack the same way he had entered the relay station. He had a six-gun in one hand and a half empty bottle of whiskey in the other, and just like before he took everyone by surprise. He let out that rebel yell I'd heard from Wash a couple of times, and if anyone in the line shack was asleep, why, they were soon very much awake.

"Howdy, folks!" he said in a brash, loud voice. He appeared to be just as drunk as he was the last time I'd seen him.

"Say, you got a lot of guts, mister," I heard one of the Wells Gang say. "You looking for trouble, are you?"

The drunken young man glanced quizzically at the gun in his hand, then at the bottle. "Naw," he said, drawing the word out with a boyish leer.

I took a few steps toward the door to our room, thinking maybe I could keep him from doing harm, the same as last time.

"You remember what I asked you to do last time, son?" I said, not sure if he'd remember me or not, what with the torn cloth bandage around my head now.

The young man cocked his head at me, studying my features for a moment while some small part of his brain that wasn't soaked with whiskey did some work. "Yeah," he said. "You asked me, real polite like. Never had that done to me much. Asking, you know."

"Then why don't you put the gun away, real nice-like," I said.

"Oh, I don't know. Look at this sorry bunch of . . ."

Almost as if she were a stage actress, Catherine stepped right up next to me in the doorway.

"Now, watch your language, son," I said. "We've got a lady here, you know," I said.

"Oh, yeah," he replied, taking in the figure of Catherine, just as he had at the relay station. "Still a pretty young lady, too." He hadn't gotten rid of the sneer yet, seeming to enjoy it, I thought.

"What about the gun?"

"Oh, sure. Sure thing," he said and twirled it around twice before holstering it.

"Thanks, son. I appreciate it," I said.

The young man nodded toward me and turned to go. Where, I had no idea. But as soon as he'd taken a couple of steps, he swung around and in a booming voice said, "I remember you! You're the daddy of them Carston brothers! That's it!"

Not that it made all that much difference. Hell, these people had all seen my badge and likely knew who I was from Bob Wells. What did make sense in an odd sort of way was this young man's claim that he knew me, for I did resemble both of my boys, or vice versa, however you want to put it. Wearing that buckskin jacket of mine likely helped, too, for Chance had one just like it, as did Wash.

"Where'd you meet my boys?" I asked out of curiosity.

"I was with your boys on that cattle drive old Charlie Goodnight and Oliver Loving made," he said. Then, sticking a hand out to me, he added, "By the way, I'm Clay Allison."

"Will Carston," I said as I took his hand.

"Yeah. Yeah, that's it." Clay Allison shook his head in what appeared to be amazement. "By God, those boys sure got a lot of respect for you, Marshal. A lot of respect. Yes, sir."

"I always figured they did."

"You'll pardon me now. I got to finish this discussion," he said and held up the bottle.

I had a sneaking idea that he was well aware of Bob Wells lifting the six-gun from his holster as Clay Allison headed for a table in the corner of the front room, sat down, and took a long pull on his half empty bottle. I could see him through the open door.

I didn't know him from Adam, this Clay Allison, but something struck me right then that, as dangerous as he seemed, it was a dangerousness I had nothing to worry about. It took a minute for my still addled mind to hit upon it, but once I sat back down on my bunk, it struck me.

This Clay Allison seemed to be acting drunk rather than actually being drunk. His words at the end, while he was telling me about Chance and Wash and the Goodnight-Loving drive, why, they were more sober than his words had been when he first entered the cabin. And he smelled like a drunk all right, but it was as though he had poured half of that bottle of whiskey on himself rather than drunk it.

So a half hour later, when he appeared to have fallen asleep, well, let's just say I had a feeling he wasn't all that much asleep.

I wasn't sure why, but something just wasn't right with that lad.

CHAPTER

★ 14 ★

This Clay Allison character was awful drunk, or playing at being awful drunk. The connecting door to the next room was open most of the day, and from what I could see of him sitting in the front room, why, he didn't move so much as a stitch the rest of that day. Hell, maybe he really was drunk. It was just that there was something about him and his appearance here that I found disturbing, to say the least. I hadn't put a pin on it yet, but it was there. That was for sure.

Come to think of it, there was an awful lot of playacting going on all around me. I'd swear that this Allison boy was playacting at being drunk, although I couldn't prove it. And Catherine Innes, why, she was real free in admitting that she was playacting the part of my sweetheart. Of course, in her case, those kisses sure did seem almighty real to me. If you know what I mean. The only ones who weren't playacting at something or other were Hank and Pardee, likely because it wasn't their style. And the Wells Gang. Hell, they couldn't do nothing but rob banks and kill people, to hear them talk. And as Mama once put it, that ain't much of a calling.

"What are you going to do with that young man?" Catherine asked one of the guards later on in the day. I reckon the motherly instinct was getting the best of her and she'd taken to fretting over the more insecure of us, at the moment it being young Clay Allison.

"Long as he sticks to his sleeping, I doubt we'll do much to him," the guard said. "He starts to fussing or acting up like he did when he first got here, there's no telling what'll happen to him."

Catherine didn't say it, but I could tell she was silently praying that young man, drunk or sober, wouldn't get involved in this mess we were in.

I found myself feeling better as the day wore on and tried spending as much time as I could in a sitting position. On occasion I even got up and walked around the room some, although I'll admit to feeling mighty light-headed after a while. Except for Clay Allison's entrance, it was the only walking about I'd done. Catherine had been taking care of my wound two or three times a day, applying more of her medicine before she replaced the bandages. It must have been salve of some sort she was spreading on my wound, the kind I'd seen in most doctors' offices, for I found it doing its job quite well, at least on me. When I asked where she'd gotten the medicines, she said

Hank had told her to pull them out of the boot of the stagecoach before they hauled everyone off. After all the shooting was over, of course.

The moon was back out that evening, showing just enough through the one lone window to spread some light across the entire room. This gave the guards an easier view of our movements, I reckon, meaning we'd be sitting ducks if we tried to escape. Not that any of us but Catherine Innes were really in any shape to do much in the line of escape. Hell, all of us men were injured in one way or another. I figured that by the time we got our bodies in motion, why, these vultures could have sighted in and killed us three times over. No, sir, we weren't in any condition to try escaping.

All of which made the feeling of desperation grow a mite more each day. We'd only been there two days, that I knew of, although I found myself wondering if I'd have gained some insight into just what did happen at that attack we'd had at the stagecoach if we'd been allowed to talk to one another. But Bob Wells had given the guards instructions not to let us converse. The lone exceptions, of course, had been Catherine Innes and myself. And that was kind of stretching it, if you ask me. Besides, the one time I did ask Catherine what had happened, she told me she was so flustered by all the shooting that she could hardly remember what had come about other than the few scraps of information she'd handed out to me about the injuries we'd all sustained. That was as far as our conversations went, unless you consider a daily kiss to be a conversation piece. There were some I knew who would do just that. I ain't that old, you know.

It was after the evening meal that Bob Wells closed

the connecting door between the rooms and had a parley with his gang in the front room, leaving only one guard to keep an eye on us. Not that he needed any more, you understand, us being all stove up like we were. I strained to hear what they might be saying but couldn't figure out what they were talking about, not for the life of me. One thing I was sure of was that part of that conversation would pertain to us and what would be done with us as prisoners or hostages or whatever you chose to call us. It gave me cause to worry, and I found myself doing that as the evening wore on.

The night went surprisingly well, and I slept soundly again, an indication of recovery, I thought. Worried as I was, I don't know how I slept, but I did. It was so peaceful that night, I'd gauge the guards even got a good night's sleep.

Catherine performed the same kind of magic with what little provisions there were and managed to stir up another decent first meal for us the next morning. But food wasn't uppermost in my mind, not now anyway.

"What's the matter, Will? My cooking isn't that bad, is it?" she asked in what I thought to be a playful manner when she saw my plate clean but my face a mite saddened.

"No, darlin'," I said in a voice that must have matched the look about me. "It ain't your cooking at all. I'm just wondering how we're gonna get out of this fix. People like this don't stay in line shacks any longer than they have to, you know. They know that someday soon that stagecoach is going to be missing on the company's schedule, and someone will start asking questions about the driver and the coach and everyone on it, you included. No, I've got a notion they're gonna be moving on soon and getting rid of us when they do."

If nothing else, she must have believed the truth in my words, for now she was looking as worried as I felt. Then a stern kind of determination came to her face, or maybe "desperation" is a better word to describe it.

"Well, we'll see about that," she said. There might have been desperation in her look, but there was pure determination in the way she picked up her skirts and marched out of our room and right into what could have been the fires of hell, for all I knew.

"Mighty pretty when she gits mad, ain't she?" Hank said, a curl of a smile forming on his lips as he spoke.

"Ain't nothing new, Hank," I said. "They all get that way when they're mad."

"I'll say." Pardee Taylor agreed. He must have been feeling better, too, for he was getting up and moving about a bit easier than when I'd first seen him lying there a day or so back. "Why, you'd think the only reason a man got his woman mad was just to see how pretty she was. Crazy institution, that marriage stuff." I didn't have to ask to know that Pardee had been listening to Chance again.

The connecting door had closed behind her when she went into the front room. I wasn't sure if it was Catherine or one of the Wells Gang who'd shut it, but like I say, she seemed to have her hands full with those skirts of hers. Once again I heard voices on the far side of that door, and once again I had trouble understanding what they were saying, even though they were loud and angry, both the woman's and the men's. Catherine Innes must have thought she was mighty persuasive as she spoke up to those yahoos, I'll give her that.

What I wasn't prepared for was the loud clap of a hand being laid across her face. I knew it was hers, for the slap was followed by a woman's scream— Catherine's scream—and the thud of a body bouncing off the wall and falling to the floor.

"Why, those dirty—" The words were as much a reflex action for my voice as it was for me to be on my feet in an instant, no matter how light-headed I might feel. Damn it, son, you just don't go around hitting women in this land! It just ain't done!

"Sit down, lawman, or you'll die where you stand," the guard said to me, a certain meanness coming out in him now that clearly made him a member of this gang with Bob Wells's name tagged on it. When I saw him jack a round into his repeating rifle and point it at my belly, I made a quick effort to follow his advice and sat down on the edge of the bed. Mad as hell, mind you, but still alive. In the back of my mind I was already making plans on how I'd take this yahoo's life.

The connecting door flew open, and Bob Wells pushed a disheveled and bruised-looking Catherine Innes into the room and on the floor. I reckon Hank, Pardee, and me were all feeling stronger than we might have thought at that moment, for the three of us were at her side in a right quick moment.

"You three get back to your places," the guard said in a loud voice. About the only thing he had going for him right now was that rifle he had trained on us, but none of us were having any of his guff now.

"You go straight to hell, you oversized jackass!" Hank said in as reckless a manner as I'd ever heard him speak.

The words threw the man, and for a blink of an eye he was flat-out confused about what to do. I reckon he figured he didn't have any options left, so he raised his rifle and took aim right at Hank's chest. "I swear to God I'll kill you, old-timer," he growled in a half-hearted way.

Hank stood up and placed his one good hand on his right hip, matching this plug-ugly look for look, word for word, if that was the way he wanted it. "Sonny, I'm too goddamn old to worry about dying, so if you think shooting an unarmed man will put another notch on your weapon, you go right ahead. This here lady needs tending to, and we aim to see she gets it, so sit down yourself and shut up, you damn pup!"

If Hank was running a bluff, he sure made the most of it, for that was just what the gutless guard did. He backed off and stayed out of our way as we picked Catherine up and carried her over to the bunk I'd been occupying.

"Damn," Pardee said under his breath in amazement after we'd laid Catherine down. "He's more reckless than I am."

"Now what you've got to do, Pardee, is try and figure out how old Hank is and whether or not you'll ever live to be that old," I said, hoping it would keep his mind fixed on something else while I tried to take care of Catherine. God only knew she deserved better help than she was getting.

Her lip had been cut, and there was a bruise under her left eye. One of those sons of bitches had not only slapped her hard but taken a fist to her face, unless she'd hit something on her way to the floor. Hell, it didn't matter to me. All it meant was I had one more reason for killing the whole bunch of them who claimed to be the Wells Gang.

102

"Bastards," I all but whispered as I dabbed the blood from Catherine's lip.

"I thought you didn't use language like that in front of a lady," Catherine said, trying ever so hard to smile through the pain I knew she was suffering.

"You'll likely hear a lot more before this is all over," I said. "Now, you just hush while I fix you up."

She did as I tried my best to be gentle with her. I reckon you've got to be knocked around and roughed up some your own self before you can really appreciate how it feels to patch up someone who looks like you've felt a time or two in your life. Mind you now, hoss, I've had to hold knives, bullets, and even arrows between my teeth while someone was patching me up, but Miss Catherine was a lot braver than I could ever be. Grunted a couple of times and maybe groaned some, but she never shed a tear or cried out like you'd expect a lady to do. Tough as could be, she was. Old Jim Bridger, he'd have been right proud of Catherine Innes.

"What the devil did you do to get beat up like that?" Pardee asked her when I was through tending to her cuts and bruises.

"I'm afraid I made the mistake of arguing with Mr. Wells about sparing our lives," Catherine said softly. "Tenderly" was a better word to describe it, I reckon. She sounded like she might have a couple of rattled teeth inside her mouth, the way she was talking.

"Don't fancy being told what to do, does he?" Hank said.

This time Catherine only nodded, although she tried like hell to smile about it. She had real gumption, this lady.

"Don't you worry," I whispered to her, hoping the guard wouldn't hear my voice. "He'll pay for it. I swear that to you."

I was already down on my knees beside her, and in that one fleeting moment I thought I'd repay her, see if I couldn't make her feel as good as she'd made me. Ever so gently I leaned over and kissed the side of her mouth that hadn't been injured.

She smiled, almost embarrassed at what I had done, I thought. Then Hank was leaning over her, too.

"I know I'm busted up, old, and ugly, ma'am," he said after kissing her on the forehead, "but you sure do remind me of a granddaughter I got back east."

What the two of us had done had taken this woman's breath away, that was for sure. But it was Pardee Taylor who really stopped us all cold.

He didn't kiss her. No, sir. He just picked up her limp hand and kissed it, just like you'd see one of those fancy stage actors do in a play. But his face was sad as could be.

"You wouldn't want to kiss an old flannelmouth like me" was all he said before turning away from her in what I was sure was shame and quietly walking off to a corner of the room to be by himself.

"Well, I'll be damned," I muttered to myself in pure surprise.

"Most of us are," Hank said.

Pardee Taylor, the bully of Twin Rifles, had finally learned an important lesson in humility. I reckon none of us knew it better than Pardee himself.

As for Catherine Innes, I knew damn good and well she knew it, for when I looked back down at her, I saw a teardrop roll down the side of her face.

CHAPTER
★ 15 ★

I was now more determined than ever either to put these sorry bastards in jail or to plant them in the ground, if you get my drift. The people in the courts would likely have wanted me to bring them in alive, but the way I was feeling I'd just as soon have used them as fertilizer for next year's crops or, if I'd had a good dose of strychnine, just leave them on the prairie and spread some of the poison over their dead bodies. Get rid of a goodly number of buzzards that do nothing but prey on the dead and dying in this land. That was how hateful I was feeling. Damn it, you don't go about hitting women in this land, and that's that! They're too precious to treat like that.

It was an hour later, and Catherine's eye had started to take on a purplish tint around the edges, as had the cheek that had been bruised. It was then I knew we weren't likely to last out the day.

The gang hadn't bothered to close the connecting door when they threw Catherine back into our room, so I had no trouble hearing what they had to say. Nor did they seem to care who heard their almighty plans. Confident bastards, these.

"Sam, it's time to leave," I heard Bob Wells tell one of his men, likely one of the guards we'd had watching over us. Just like I'd figured, they wouldn't stay around any longer than they had to. It wasn't this crowd's way of doing things. Like I said, all they seemed to be any good at was killing people and robbing banks. And you know what Mama said about that.

"What do you want me to do, boss?" Sam asked. I could see the rest of the Wells Gang filing outdoors through the front door of the line shack as their boss gave instructions to Sam.

"We got their guns, and the men are all stove up except for that passed-out drunk, so they shouldn't be any problem for you," Wells said with confidence.

"You want me to—"

"Kill 'em, just like that bunch we took up in Kansas after our last bank job," Wells said. I couldn't see his face, but the way he said it left me with no doubt that he had a sneer on his face. "Scatter the bodies around so it looks like they were fighting about something. Leave an empty pistol in one of their hands and a bullet hole in each of the rest. Leave 'em dead, Sam. Just leave 'em dead."

"I'll get it done, boss," Sam said. He must have taken great pleasure in killing people by the look of him. Acted like it was an everyday ordinary thing for him. I purely hate those types. It's one of the reasons I took this job of being a lawman. "Give me an hour or so and I'll catch up with you."

"See you later," Bob Wells said, and then he was gone.

I heard them gallop off and made my way to the window, feeling a mite faint once I got there for the rushing I'd done. I couldn't swear to it, but I do believe they had about half a dozen men in their gang now. At first it didn't make much sense, for I thought I'd counted a bit more than that during the attempted bank robbery at Twin Rifles, and knew we'd shot at least one out of the saddle. Then I'd seen one—or was it two?—fall when they attacked the stagecoach. I hadn't recalled seeing any wounded men, for all of the guards had been in healthy shape, so if the ones I'd seen fall were indeed dead, why, the Wells Gang had picked up an extra man or two along the way. Of course, at the moment I didn't really care if it was two hundred of them in that gang. All I knew was that I'd hunt them down to the ends of the earth if that was what it took to be rid of them.

Still, getting out of this pickle was going to be a real chore. Bob Wells had been right. They had all of our guns and Hank, Pardee and me weren't in too good a shape to try taking the rifle and six-gun away from the one man left to guard us, the one who also intended to kill us. How in the hell were we going to get out of this?

"You all right, darlin'?" I asked Catherine as I sat down beside her.

She gave me a faint but painful smile. Good girl, I thought to myself. "I'll be all right, Will. I'll be fine once we get out of here."

107

I was having a great deal of respect for this young lady, more and more as the days went on. And, hoss, that's saying something.

I patted her hand, hoping it would give her some kind of reassurance. "It won't be long now, darlin', it won't be long now at all." I just didn't tell her that getting out of this line shack, getting out of the mess we were in, might well entail dying. It was an alternate I wasn't too keen on recognizing. But then, nobody ever is.

It's amazing how your body will tell you things just in the nick of time. You know what I mean—that feeling you get in your stomach when you can't prove it but you just *know* you're about to ride into a valley full of Comanches. The way the hair stands up on the back of your neck when you know for certain that trouble is coming your way. Things like that. Well, hoss, I had the damnedest itch on the back of my neck, and I reckon it was that itch that gave me a breath of hope.

It was then I felt the rawhide thong that hung around my neck, the rawhide thong that hardly anyone could see or know was there unless they took a real close look. The rawhide strip that held a tinker's knife in a small sheath that hung inside my shirt just below my collar. The small knife barely fit in my fist, but that didn't matter. It was balanced for throwing, and that was the important thing. With one well-placed throw I could do away with this son of a bitch holding us hostage. The trouble was, I wasn't sure I had the strength to make the throw I would need in order to put an end to this outlaw's life rather than my own. But this wasn't a time to be cautious. Not by a long sight.

"Pardee," I said in a whisper to the man across Catherine's bunk from me, "I'm gonna need your help."

It must have been the first time Pardee Taylor had ever heard me ask for his help, and he was all for doing what he could. This time I hoped he'd do what *I* told him and not what Chance had told him. Sometimes Chance could be a real bother to me, whether he was my son or not.

"Name it," he said in just as low a voice. I reckon he had an idea what we had to do to get out of here. Maybe the lad wasn't so set in his ways after all.

"You walk off to that corner, like you did earlier, as though you were wanting to be left alone," I said in a whisper. Pardee nodded, understanding. "Then you sort of sidle along the side wall toward the connecting doorway, where that guard is standing." The man had placed himself in the doorway, leaning half in our room and half in the front room, wanting to keep one eye on us and the other on Clay Allison, who still appeared to be asleep in the other room. He'd have his back toward one of us when Pardee made his way toward him against the wall. "I'm gonna try killing him, and soon as I do he's gonna trying doing in at least one of us. That's when I want you to grab the barrel of his rifle and hold on for all your life."

"I'll do it," Pardee whispered and began to move away toward the corner of the room, just as I'd instructed him to.

Pardee Taylor, the town bully of Twin Rifles, was doing a lot of growing up of late. Fact of the matter was, I could see a lot of improvement in the lad in the past twenty-four hours.

Pardee was only halfway along the side wall when

Sam, our executioner, pulled his rifle down to hip level and pointed it toward me, Hank, and Catherine. "All right, folks, it's time to say good-bye," he said with a crooked leer that told me he was going to enjoy this even more than I'd thought. Then he pulled back the hammer of his rifle.

It was then I thought I saw a figure behind him in the other room. I could only hope that my thoughts about Clay Allison had been right—that he had indeed been playacting like a drunken cowboy, that he was about to save our bacon, that he was giving me the time and the chance to come out of this mess alive.

He never did get the chance.

The front door to the line shack flew open, and in stepped Dallas Bodeen, his Henry rifle in hand. Young Clay Allison had been standing right inside the front door, and when Dallas busted in, the door had slammed up against young Allison, knocking him nearly across the room and to the floor as it hit him.

"Fill your hand!" Dallas yelled at the man standing before him. And that was just what old Sam intended to do. He had turned his back to that front door, intent on killing us, you understand. But he must have figured taking care of this intruder wouldn't be a problem at all. He had to bring his rifle up to port arms, if my military terminology is still correct, and then bring it down to do in Dallas, even though he did have the rifle cocked and ready to fire. What he didn't realize was that he was giving Dallas all the time in the world to do just what my old friend wanted to do.

By the time Sam was turned around and bringing his rifle down on Dallas, he'd already taken a slug high in the chest. The bullet threw him back into our room as he pulled the trigger on his rifle, and the shot went wild up through the ceiling. But while all that was happening, I'd pulled out my tinker's knife and thrown it square in his back. Mind you, hoss, I never was for shooting or knifing a man in the back, but I'll tell you flat out that when it comes to my life or his, well, I don't really give a damn how it is I take his life. He fell onto his back, the force of his deadweight driving the knife that much farther into his back so that if Dallas's bullet didn't kill him, my knife did.

Pardee Taylor grabbed the rifle from the man's hands as he fell to his death.

"You touch that bottle, I'll kill you too, sonny!" Dallas growled at Clay Allison, jacking another round into the chamber of his Henry rifle.

"Don't!" I yelled, trying to step over the dead man before me. "He's on our side . . . I think."

Young Clay Allison had been reaching for the bottle he'd dropped when the door had slammed into him, knocking him flat on his ass.

"That's right, mister," Clay said, a mite angry at being thrown down on. "Why, I was ready to bust this whiskey bottle over that fella's head." The way he said it seemed as though Dallas and I had spoiled all the fun he was going to have doing what he'd planned. "Hell, yes, I'm on your side."

"I got the rifle, Marshal," Pardee said behind me, and I turned to see him holding the weapon up in one hand to show me, like a proud son talking to his father about a new accomplishment.

And I was proud, for it reminded me of Wash and Chance and some of the same sort of days I'd had with them so long ago.

I smiled at him. "You done fine, Pardee, just fine."

"Thanks, Marshal. Thanks."

"Say, Pardee."

"Yes, sir."

"It's okay if you call me Will now. Most of the rest of the folks in Twin Rifles do. I won't get mad at you—promise."

"Yes, sir. I'll do that."

From the look of him, I'd say Pardee Taylor had just gained back a hell of a lot of his lost pride.

CHAPTER
★ 16 ★

"And just who the hell might you be?" Dallas growled, still holding his Henry rifle on Clay Allison. Dallas had a way of losing trust in damn near everyone when he got into a shooting situation, as I recall. Everyone except the people he could really call his friends, and he didn't know the young man before him at all. No, sir.

"I wouldn't be so nervous about explaining myself if I didn't have to look into the business end of that rifle, friend," young Allison said in a voice that showed it.

"Why don't you give that Henry of yours a rest, compadre," Blacksnake Hank said, appearing in the doorway behind me. "I'll grant you I've got a busted-

113

up arm, but it never took me more than one hand to use one of these." Apparently Hank had grabbed up the six-gun belonging to our now dead executioner. He held it up to show Dallas what he was talking about, then backed into a chair off to the side, the six-gun resting on his lap, still firmly in his grip. "You fellas need to get this thing straightened out. You leave the shooting to me for a mite."

"Sounds good to me," Clay Allison said as he brushed off his pants, grabbed his own hat, and plunked it down on the back of his head. The way he was talking, why, he didn't seem anywhere close to drunk. Not now, anyway.

"Never mind him, Dallas," I said. "Just how is it you showed up out of nowhere? I don't recall you doing that for some time now."

"Used to be one of my specialties, ary you'll recall," he said with a smile.

"I wouldn't say you're too far out of practice, friend," I said in appreciation of what he'd done. You don't take a man saving your life in a light manner. If he's your friend, you'd damn sure better not make light of it if you want to keep him as a friend. "But that don't answer my question, Dallas."

"Well, it's like this, Will," Dallas said and went on to tell us that he'd had a conversation with Rachel back in Twin Rifles. Margaret Ferris was worried about me, he said, and she had the silly notion that Catherine Innes was some kind of threat to her. "Me, I had a notion that something had happened to you, too, Will, only I wasn't worried about no femme fatale, if you get my drift." He glanced past me at Catherine, who had gotten up from the bunk as soon as the shooting started and had the good sense to stay

114

out of sight until it stopped. It seemed that just about everyone had moved from that back room to the front room of the line shack now, including Catherine. "Although I can see why Miss Margaret might have had some concerns," Dallas added, taking in Catherine's features with a smile.

"I'm flattered, sir," Catherine said with a smile, a bit of a blush crawling up her face.

"Oh, you don't want to call me sir, ma'am," Dallas replied. "I work for a living."

"Dallas never was one for getting his work done in the shade, Catherine," I said, hoping that would explain it all.

"I understand." I didn't know how she could keep up a smile like that, but she did. Yes, sir, I was getting a whole lot of respect for this young lady.

"Anyway," Dallas continued, "I sit there a-thinking how there wasn't a thing I could do for you, me being in Twin Rifles and you on that stagecoach." Dallas paused a moment to shake his head in disbelief. With an embarrassed smile, he added, "I must be getting old. Took me all of ten minutes after I left the Ferris House to remember what I've been telling all of those young bucks over the years."

"Oh, what's that?" Clay Allison said. Dallas always was a good storyteller, and he'd definitely caught young Allison's interest.

"Why, there's *always* something you can do!" Dallas blurted out, as though pointing out a fact as plain as the nose on your face.

"True enough," Allison said with a nod of his head.

"That was when I put together my possibles bag and began trailing that stagecoach. When I come on it and seen what happened, why, I knew you was in trouble and just followed the tracks. I've got to tell you, these birds sure didn't try covering their trail," he said.

"Well, you saved my bacon, hoss," I said, giving my old riding pard a slap on the back.

"And how many times is it I've done that now?" he asked, a curious look about him.

"We won't go into that right now," I said in what must have been a humble tone.

"Which brings me to my original question," Dallas said, turning his attention to young Allison. "Just how is it you wound up here?"

Clay Allison, it seemed, had sobered up back at the relay station I'd first met him at, and still had it in his mind that he knew me from somewhere. He got his guns back and decided to follow the stagecoach, although he was a couple of hours behind us.

"Like the old-timer says, I got to that stagecoach, and it wasn't hard to figure out that you folks were in trouble," Allison said. "By then I'd figured out you looked a heap like those Carston boys on that cattle drive last year." Here the young man shrugged as he thought of the right words to say. "They done their jobs well, and we got along fine, so I figured maybe I'd lend a hand if you really was in a fix. Acting like a drunken fool seemed about the safest way of getting into their camp to find out what was going on. As for the trail, why, I could have been as drunk as a lord and still followed it." Again young Allison was silent, running some thoughts through his mind. Finally, in a hesitant tone of voice, he said to me, "Besides, you were decent to me. So were your boys. I like that in a man."

"I know what you mean," I said. I stuck my hand

out to him in case he wanted to accept it. "I'm glad you did come this far. I like that in a man, too."

"Well, we'd better get going after 'em, then," Clay Allison said, as though everyone should know some deep dark secret.

"What for?" Pardee asked.

"While I was laying over there supposedly sleeping, I heard 'em talking amongst themselves," Allison said.

"Is that a fact?" Dallas said. "Anything interesting come of it?"

"I think so."

"And what might that be?"

"You from a place called Twin Rifles, Marshal?" the young man asked.

"Yes."

"This gang, they try to rob your bank a while back?"

"That's a fact, son. Weren't none too successful at it, though. Mostly they got away with their lives more than any of our money."

"Then I didn't hear 'em wrong."

"And what is it you didn't hear wrong?" Dallas said with a cocked eyebrow.

"I reckon they don't like failure," Clay Allison said. "They said they were heading back to clean the bank out."

117

CHAPTER

★ 17 ★

W**ell now, what do you think about that?"** Dallas said in mild astonishment. It wasn't like Dallas Bodeen to be astonished at anything.

"I'd say saddle and ride, hoss, saddle and ride," Clay Allison said.

"I'd like to see that," Catherine Innes said in a tone that had changed from the ease of a laugh to pure defiance.

"Begging your pardon, ma'am, but do you want to run that by my trail one more time?" Hank said in his own determined voice. "I think I missed the coach on that one."

Catherine Innes's eyes got as wide as any child's on Christmas morn, black eye or not. And I do believe her head shot back with the same kind of denial that was in her voice. "Well, look at you! Look at the lot of you! There's not a one of you fit to ride or fight!" she said with a good deal of authority. If she was a schoolteacher, I had a notion she was a right good one. Yes, sir. "Except for the young man—Allison, I believe his name is—and the older man, Dallas what's-his-name."

I took a slow inventory of the crowd in the room now. Me, I had a head that had a bad habit of getting light on me if I went too far too fast on it. Pardee Taylor had a busted-in side and walked about as tender as my head felt. Blacksnake Hank had a flat-out busted arm that didn't keep him in much more than a mood for cussing. I could see it in his face. As for Sam, our would-be executioner, why, he wasn't going nowhere unless it was the fiery gates of hell. Wasn't in any shape to, truth to tell. So Catherine Innes was right, we'd likely get laughed at one hell of a lot before the Wells Gang got around to killing us on a permanent basis.

"That might be, Miss Catherine, but it don't mean I can't try," I said. There comes a time when, bad off as you feel, you do what has to be done. "If I don't go after those yahoos, why, I'll have to turn my badge in to the city council of Twin Rifles. Wouldn't be worth a damn to them or me. No, ma'am." I ran a hand across my jaw, trying to think of something more meaningful to say and having a hard time finding the right words. "Besides," I finally said, coming up with the only words that made sense, the only words that fit at the time, "Dallas was right. Everyone's got a choice. And I ain't sitting on my git-up end to wait for the Wells Gang to stop robbing banks. You can bet your . . . bottom dollar on that!"

"Now you're talking, Will," Pardee said, which is about what I expected him to say. Hell, the lad would agree with the devil himself if it meant he'd get on his good side. You'd think he was desperate for friends or something, which may not have been far from the truth. To Catherine he said, "If you can wrap this side of mine up a mite tighter, why, I do believe I'll make it to the ball, ma'am."

"Don't you boys go a-counting me out," Hank said in a firm voice. "I need to get hold of those yahoos worse than all the rest of you."

"I don't know, mister," Dallas said, "that arm looks pretty bad to me."

"What is it you got against these pilgrims?" Clay Allison asked. "You must've been held up a time or two on the line. What makes this so special?"

"Why, the sons a bitches *killed all my horses!*" Hank exploded in a voice as filled with hatred as any I've ever heard. Hank had a real love for those animals, got along real well with them, he did. Taking their lives was almost the same as shooting one of your blood kin, he felt that strongly about them.

Remembering how we'd been kept from speaking to one another, I glanced at Dallas and raised an eyebrow, silently seeking the verification of the stagecoach driver's words.

"Oh, he's right, Will," Dallas said. "When I come across them horses, they wasn't fit for no one but a coyote or an army cook, and I do believe the coyote would have passed them over."

"Well, if you three think you can make it, I'm coming, too," Catherine said, the authority creeping back into her voice. When Pardee, Hank, and me just looked at one another in wonderment, then gave her a frown, she added, "I don't like being pushed around by bullies the likes of your Wells Gang."

And that was that. Not that we didn't have a few looks from Dallas and the Allison youth that said we were totally crazy, you understand.

"You boys need some rest," Dallas said with a shake of his head. "Why, you're not only ailing, you ain't got no weaponry that I can see."

But like it or not the three of us were determined to go after them.

"I got this," Pardee said, holding up the rifle he'd taken off of Sam when the man was shot dead. "This feller ain't gonna be needing it."

"Me, I prefer a shotgun," Hank said, hefting the six-gun he'd taken from Sam's holster, "but this thing'll kill as good as any, I reckon."

Me, I didn't have nothing except the holster I'd carried my Remington in. That and the tinker's knife, which was still in Sam's back. Truth to tell, I felt downright embarrassed about not having a weapon of some sort to fend off the Wells Gang with. But I reckon Dallas was getting back in the habit of saving the day.

"I always did favor a rifle, Will," he said, lifting the Henry in his hand as though to balance the rifle. "Got an extry Colt in the saddlebags ary I run outta ammunition for this thing. I'll let you borrow it temporary."

"Thanks," I said, hoping he knew how much I really did appreciate his helping out. But that was Dallas.

This time it was Clay Allison who had a reddish color creeping up his neck. "Looks like I'm the only one ain't got a six-gun," he said in a humble manner.

"That bay out in the wooded area yours?" Dallas asked.

"Yeah. Why do you ask?"

"It 'pears to me I seen a belt, holster, and pistol hanging from the saddle horn," Dallas said.

Clay Allison gave out a sigh of relief and was out the door in a flash, likely heading for his horse and his fighting gear.

That gave us all one gun each. Whether or not it was a good enough match for going up against Bob Wells and his gang I wasn't sure. Normally I'd say it was all a matter of shooting, but at the moment, as light as my head was feeling, I just wasn't sure.

Dallas Bodeen shook his head as he took in the lot of us. "I still think I'm the only one who come prepared here," he said with a growl that went straight back to the Rocky Mountains and those years so long ago when I'd first met him.

But just between you and me, I had a notion he was right.

CHAPTER

★ 18 ★

The pleasant smile on Clay Allison's face when he came back in was the only indication I needed that Dallas had been right about his six-gun, belt, and holster being on his horse outside. Of course, force of habit made me glance at his side to make sure I wasn't imagining things.

Catherine went to work at the potbellied stove, gathering up what little bits of food the Wells Gang had left behind. I reckon they were living off the land like many a man did these days. Either that or they had as little taste for the food we'd been eating as me and the rest did. I mean, Catherine did a right fine job of making it all edible when she was cooking, but there's just so much you can do with that kind of a meal, just so many times you can eat it. I remembered

123

Chance and Wash bellyaching about the lack of variety in their meals not long ago, when they'd returned from that cattle drive.

"Now, how many times is that I've saved your ass?" Dallas asked outside as he dug into his saddlebag, produced a Colt 1860 Army Model in .44 caliber, and handed it to me butt first. The sly smile on his face told me he was going to have some fun with our past history.

Me, I wasn't having any of it. "We won't talk about that right now, Dallas" was my reply. I hefted the six-gun in my hand, trying to get the feel of it. It was almost the same as my Remington, although I much preferred the Remington. Chance was the one who was crazy about these Colt revolvers. Something about them that seemed to fit his personality, if that can be said.

"Well, why not, Will? Hell, I saved your bacon oncet today, then went on to keep you from being downright humiliated, not having a six-gun and all when everyone else did, you being a lawman and all," he said with a chuckle.

"It's like this, old hoss," I said to the man standing directly in front of me. "This gunshot wound to my head has pretty much done in my sense of humor, so I reckon you can understand when I say that, first off, I'd rather be in more pleasant circumstances when you and I go over the past. Second," I added, glancing down at the Colt in my hand before looking back at Dallas, "I'd rather have a beer in my hand than a fully loaded six-gun, you understand. Why, this weapon might go off by accident and shoot someone, me being so light-headed and all."

It didn't take Dallas long to catch on.

"Oh, I understand, Will," he said, suddenly eager to please a delirious old friend. "Understand perfectly. You're coming right along, Will, right along," he said with a smile that was as fake as the front of Ernie Johnson's saloon, then patted me softly on the arm as he hastily vacated the area. Not that I could ever swear to it, you understand, but I do believe I heard old Dallas mutter something along the lines of "crotchety old bastard" under his breath as he left.

Of course I was only half joshing the man in what I'd said. The day was only half done, and already I was feeling mighty tired, like an old man who should be taking an afternoon siesta. Too bad we weren't in Mexico where I could have gotten away with it. Yes, sir. But I'd told this bunch that I had to go after these yahoos, basically because they'd interfered with the performance of my job, which was getting their leader, Bob Wells, to Fort Dodge for trial. "Obstruction of justice" is how they put it in those fancy black books, the ones they've got the laws and all written down in. That was the reason I had for going after them, no matter what kind of shape I was in. I might die along the way, but unless I did my damnedest to put Wells and his gang out of business, well, like I said, I wouldn't be worth much to the town or to my own self. And a man who ain't no good to himself, why, he's about as useless as a man afoot in the desert. No, I had to go after them, light-headed feeling or not.

Dallas turned out to be full of surprises.

"Say, how'd you get hold of that mount of mine?" Pardee asked when Dallas had disappeared briefly into the wooded area that surrounded the line shack and returned with Pardee's mount and mine.

"Yeah, where'd you come up with mine?" I asked

the same question as Pardee. I'd completely forgotten that I'd had my own horse tied behind the stagecoach on this trip, figuring on taking my own sweet time riding back to Twin Rifles once my mission was completed. I reckon that's what head wounds will do to a man.

"Truth to tell, I ain't rightly sure," Dallas said, scratching his head. "When I come on that coach you was supposed to be on, I seen all those tracks circling the coach, and I understood the way they'd attacked you. But once I rode outside of that circle, why, the only tracks I found that didn't bunch up and ride off in one direction was these two horses. They ran off in the opposite direction, and I recognized your horse's tracks, Will, so I followed 'em until I caught up with these two horses. Only thing I can figure is they got scared off by that gunfire or they was cut loose."

"Don't matter, I reckon," I said as I inspected my horse to see if any harm had come to him. It hadn't, so I said a silent prayer of thanks and counted my blessings. Mama said that didn't do no harm every once in a while. Figured it kept a body mortal, she did. I do believe she was right.

That meant two of us would have to ride double, Hank and Catherine. Pardee said he'd take on Hank, while I had Catherine for a riding partner. In both cases the riders pretty much fit, I thought. Hank and Pardee both had busted-up bones, so neither one would complain about the other not going fast enough, of that I was sure. As for me, I never had fancied riding double with anyone on a horse, figuring it tended to work them out that much faster. Still, I wasn't about to go galloping off on a trail like a hound after a rabbit he's scented. Not with this head. So taking it easy first out was fine with me, even if it did feel sort of strange having Catherine in back of me once we got going. Or maybe it was just the guilty feeling that somewhere, somehow, Margaret knew what was going on. And when I say Margaret Ferris is good with her pots and pans, I'm not just talking about her cooking skills.

Sam, our would-be executioner, was draped across his saddle. Dallas agreed that I shouldn't leave the man here to be discovered and hauled in by someone else. "What if there's a bounty on him?" he asked. Money was still scarce in Texas, and people who had it were even scarcer, if you get my drift. And the fact of the matter was that Dallas had indeed killed the man, so if there was a bounty on him—which there likely was if he was one of the Wells Gang—I'd rather see it go to Dallas Bodeen than some saddle bum who happened on a dead man in a line shack. So I reckon you could say that Sam rode his own horse out of there, in a manner of speaking.

Off we went, Dallas and young Clay Allison riding hard to our front, doing what tracking they could and then waiting for us to catch up with them. Come to think of it, I wouldn't have doubted it if they'd reached the site we camped at close to sundown and been there several hours before we caught up with them. But they did have coffee and some prairie chicken on the fire when we caught up with them, which wasn't long before sunset that day. Don't ask me how far we went that day, for I'm not at all sure my mind was working that well. All I knew was that I was dead tired and sure could have used a siesta that afternoon rather than sit in a saddle under what seemed like the grueling heat of the day.

"Thought you'd never make it," Dallas said with a know-it-all grin when Pardee and Hank and Catherine and me rode into camp.

"Man ought not be riding in heat like this," Clay Allison said, the same kind of look on his face.

"You mean a horse ought not to be out in weather like this," I replied, acting awful tired my own self but determined not to be taken in by their joshing. "I'm just stopping to give these horses a rest. Hell, they been doing all the work." Which was true. A man riding across a far piece of land acts like he's been plowing a Missouri farmer's field when he lights down from his mount, but the truth of the matter is, it's his horse that's been doing most of the work. And let's face it, mules don't look nothing like humans, although I've seen more than a couple of both species that sure do act the same way.

The food, as small a portion as it was, did me good, as did the coffee. But it couldn't stop me from wanting to take just a little bit of a nap, as tired as I was.

"You boys wake me up in about half an hour or so, you hear?" I said, feeling a mite of the authority returning to my voice. Maybe I was getting better after all. "As I recall, there should be at least part of a moon out tonight, so we can keep on tracking these buzzards through the night."

"You bet, Marshal," Allison said, pulling out his six-gun and checking the rounds in it. It crossed my mind that the boy might come in right handy after all.

I was about to lie down when I saw Catherine give off a shiver, which wasn't unusual, this being late fall and the sun not far from setting anyway. It was about time for a breeze to pick up and cut the heat of the day, as I recalled.

"Here you go, darlin'," I said. I took off my oversized buckskin jacket and handed it to her.

"Thanks, Will," she said in that sweet way she had. Even with that black eye there was no denying the beauty of the woman.

"Remember what I said, boys," I said as I lay down off to the side. "No more than an hour."

CHAPTER
★ 19 ★

I dreamed about Cora when I dropped off to sleep, just as I'd done a number of times since her death. Strange as it might seem, each time I did dream of the woman I'd been married to for the better part of my life, it had been about a different part of our life together. This time the dream was about our early days, when she and I were so in love with each other, and our parents were so against the whole idea of us sharing a life together. It wasn't until some years later, while reading some of that Shakespeare's writings in the mountains, that it crossed my mind that our situation in those early days of our love wasn't much different than that Romeo and Juliet couple Shakespeare had written about. Not so different at all.

We'd finally run away from all of them, figuring it

was time to start thinking about ourselves instead of what our respective families were wanting of us. I'll never forget that first night we spent alone next to a cold campfire. It wasn't the warmest part of the year, and we huddled together to keep from freezing. I could still remember it. She crawled in between me and the remains of the fire that night, cozying up to my back while the fire kept her own back warm for a while. She threw her arm and part of a blanket over me, doing her best to share with me what she had. Oh, it was cold that night, but I slept well, knowing that Cora was there beside me. My dream reminded me an awful lot of Cora and that first night, an awful lot.

When I woke up, I was lying on my side, just as I had when I'd lain down an hour ago. Except it wasn't an hour ago. Not hardly! It was still a mite dark, but you'd better believe I ain't so goddamn old I don't know the difference between first light and last light, and, mister, it was first light I was seeing!

My cheeks and my chest were kind of cold, but my back awful warm. For that one instant it takes you to run everything through your mind and figure out what in the hell is going on, I froze. Comanches? No, I'd been through that experience before, and they weren't that quiet once you woke up. Wells and his gang? Maybe. They sure knew we were stove up enough to not be much of a threat to them. Then I felt movement on my chest and wondered if it wasn't a gila monster come all the way from down Arizona way that was taking a hold of me. Slowly I moved my hand over to where I thought this animal was and grabbed a hold of it. It only took a second to realize that what I'd taken hold of wasn't a gila monster or anything else all that dangerous. It was a hand. A small hand. A woman's hand. Just like my Cora's hand so many years ago. But Cora was dead. . . .

"Catherine?" I said in what must have been an obfusticated tone of voice.

"Please, Will, you're hurting my hand," I heard her whisper as she pulled it away.

"Sorry," I said in my most humble voice. Here I was doing what I was most against, harming a woman. "I didn't mean . . ." I started to say as I turned to face her, my head not that far off the ground.

"It's all right," she said. Then she took hold of my face and kissed me. I'll admit to enjoying it at first, although the remembrance that we were still in a camp and there were other people present put a quick damper on any enjoyment I was having.

"No, it's not all right," I said once I tore myself away from her.

"I don't know, friend, I'd take it where I could get it," I heard young Clay Allison say off to the side. "Why, I recall places you'd have to put a burlap sack over a woman's head to kiss her, she was that ugly. But Miss Catherine here—"

"Damn it, you were supposed to wake me up after an hour!" I said, not caring at the moment who heard what I said or how I said it.

"Don't blame me, Marshal," Allison said, holding a hand up as though to ward off a blow. "Your friend Dallas and this young filly decided you were in need of rest. Hell, we were all in need of rest last night, us and the horses. Must be after five or so now."

"Don't be mad, Will," Catherine said, sitting up and taking my hand. "It was for your own good, you know. Really." She gave off a smile like I used to see on my mother's face when she was trying to be stern and sweet at the same time.

"What the—" I heard Dallas say as he grabbed up his Henry and rolled over, pointing it in my direction. "Oh, you," he said and lay back on his bedroll.

"That's right, Dallas. It's me, the crotchety old bastard," I said with a growl as I remembered his words from the previous day.

"And I want you folks to know he was *worse than this* when we was up in the mountains trapping thirty, forty years ago," Dallas said, throwing his bedding aside and waking up the rest of the camp.

"I think it's time for breakfast, gentlemen," said Catherine, ever the peacemaker. She began moving about, grabbing up the coffee pot and inspecting the canteens for some water while Allison tossed a couple of pieces of deadwood on the dying embers of the fire. Me, I tromped off out of camp, supposedly looking for more deadwood.

Actually, the night's worth of sleep had done me a world of good if the way I was feeling meant anything. I found that when I stood up I wasn't as light-headed as I'd been the day before. I felt more like I knew I was supposed to be feeling, felt like a man again. But Dallas would have a fit if he saw me acting any other way than crotchety after what had just happened, so I thought I'd string him along. Hell, he'd think I was going soft or something if I'd acted otherwise. So when I walked into camp half an hour later, I just tossed a fistful of firewood down by the campfire and grumbled something under my breath. It was enough for Dallas, if that grin I saw on him was any indication.

Catherine managed to fry some bacon Dallas had brought along, which she served up along with a biscuit for each of us. With a cup of coffee and some grease to sop up, it wasn't a half bad meal, although I'd rather have been eating a good steak at the Ferris House. Still, you learn not to complain too much after this many years.

"Got a place over on the Washita," Clay Allison said after quickly gobbling down his morning eats. If he meant the Washita River, he could be talking about an area that ran all the way from the Red River clear up into the Indian Territory north of Texas. "Started me a small place over there after the war was over."

"What brought you over this way?" I asked, feeling a mite edgy about asking such a question. I knew that there were places you could get shot for asking such a question. Just mind your own business was the rule in this area. It was one of the easier ways to stay alive.

Clay Allison simply shrugged, a boyish grin on his face. "Just get the urge to wander some times, I reckon."

"Do it with a bottle tucked in your back pocket, I see," Hank said in his tactless manner. Looking back and forth between the two, I came to the conclusion that Clay Allison and Blacksnake Hank were a lot more alike than they'd ever admit or know. Hank was just too old to give a damn what anybody thought of what he said or didn't say. Clay Allison, why, he was too damn young to know better.

"Sometimes," the lad admitted with a smile.

He was somewhere around Wash's age, maybe in his mid-twenties, although he didn't give a year of birth. He'd been in a handful of Confederate units during the war, which could be taken a number of ways.

Either a good many of the men in his unit got shot up and what was left was attached to another unit, or he was a bad enough soldier to not be wanted by any of the units he joined. Or he could have been a deserter. Not that I was going to speculate on any of those three possibilities. Hell, my own boys had been in four years' worth of war each. It had been over for a couple of years now, and they still didn't talk all that much about it. But then, I was in the Mexican War and I don't recall voluntarily telling that many tales about what I did in that war, either. I reckon war is like that.

Half an hour later we broke camp and saddled up, ready to ride. I was feeling a whole lot better today and really thought we might be able to catch up with these yahoos.

"I wish we had another horse," I said out loud as I mounted up and pulled Catherine up behind me.

"What's the matter? Don't you like your current riding partner?" Catherine asked with what I knew was a leer, although I couldn't see her face, behind me like she was.

"With all due respect to your beauty, Catherine, I've got a job to do first, and it needs getting done," I said, letting her know that, no matter how well she kissed, I still meant business.

"I'll remember you said that," she whispered in my ear.

"I'm sure you will, darlin'," I said as I jogged my horse forward. "I'm sure you will."

CHAPTER

★ 20 ★

Dallas Bodeen and young Clay Allison had lit a shuck that morning, riding off quickly and quietly on the trail of the Wells Gang as they left Will Carston, Pardee Taylor, Blacksnake Hank, and the woman, Catherine Innes, behind. There was no telling how far behind the bank robbers they were now. They might have had a three-, maybe four-hour head start when they left the line shack the day before, but God only knew how much of a head start they had now.

"What do you think?" Clay Allison asked as Dallas sifted through the ashes of a recent fire. As near as he could figure, they'd been on the trail a good three hours before coming on the dead fire.

"Colder than grandma's hindmost," Dallas said in a grim tone of voice, with a face to match.

"Ain't knew a woman yet that had a cold ass," young Allison said, acting as though this were some game he was having fun at.

Dallas Bodeen gave Clay Allison a serious glance as he looked the boy straight in the eyes and said, "Well, that's how they get after they been dead for thirty years, *sonny.*"

The young gunman immediately knew he'd said the wrong thing to the wrong man at the wrong time.

"Oh. I see," he said in a toned-down version of his until now frivolous attitude.

"If they made camp, they broke it sometime early in the night, I'd gauge," Dallas said, going back to studying the situation.

"Sounds like they made good use of what little moon there is to git where they were going." Clay Allison suddenly seemed to be taking on a more serious disposition in this matter.

"That or they knew exactly where they were heading," Dallas said, pushing his hat back and giving his graying hair a scratch before lowering his hand.

"You thinking what I'm thinking?" the young gunman said, picking up on what he thought to be the obvious conclusion.

"If Will was right and these are the fellers who tried robbing his bank, I'd say at least one of 'em was watching his back trail when they left town that day." He paused a moment, looking in the direction the trail led. Nodding his head, he added, "Yup, they're heading back to Twin Rifles all right."

"Think we can catch 'em?"

"Ary we don't," Dallas said, mounting his horse, "at least we'll be a far piece closer than we are sitting on our duffs now."

With those words, Dallas Bodeen kicked his horse's sides and lit out on the trail the Wells Gang had plainly left for them to follow. He couldn't help but wonder if they weren't as bad at hiding a trail as they seemed to be at robbing banks. Or were they leaving a trail to follow with the idea in mind of doing in anyone who had a notion to follow them? Unless, of course, old Sam back at the line shack couldn't read sign any better than he could defend himself and they wanted to make sure he caught up with the gang. Nothing like having your own personal executioner with you to do the dirty work.

It took Clay Allison a while to catch up to the man, although, as he'd once put it, he could have been dead drunk and still been able to follow that trail. He, too, had questions about the Wells Gang running through his mind, and they weren't all that different from what Dallas Bodeen found himself wondering.

The land they were doing this tracking in was a combination of dry, arid stretches of near desert-like terrain that ran into clumps of forest where water could be found. At the rate they were travel-ing, Clay Allison wondered if Dallas Bodeen was keeping an eye out for water as much as he was the trail of the Wells Gang. Even the greenest greenhorn, if he'd made it this far west, was versed enough in the art of staying alive to know that a man with-out a horse was no man at all. So a smart man, no matter what his objective was, kept an eye out for the water holes in the area he was traveling, at least if he wanted to keep traveling that area for any length of time.

Later on in the afternoon Clay Allison caught up

with Dallas Bodeen, watering his horse near a grove of cottonwoods.

"I wondered if you'd ever stop near a watering hole," young Allison said as he reined in his mount. He appeared to be almost as out of breath as his horse, which brought a chuckle from Dallas at the sight of the young man and his horse.

"I can see I'm gonna have to tell you about the days me and Will spent as trappers up in the Shinin' Mountains and out here as Texas Rangers," Dallas said with a smile and a not-so-humble tone of voice as the young man and his horse took their fill of water.

"You know, I never could figure that out," Clay Allison said, wiping a forearm across his mouth.

"What's that?" Dallas asked.

"All the old-timers I come across got nothing better to do than tell stories. Talk and talk is all they do."

"Oh, that's easy to figure out, son," Dallas said with a confident smile. "Of course, you being a young 'un, it's still a mystery to you."

Clay Allison's expression turned into a frown of confusion. "You want to run that by me one more time?"

"Why, us old farts has been around long enough to have a whole passel of stories to tell," Dallas said, as though revealing the secret to the whereabouts of lost gold. "Makes us want to laugh at you young squirts, wet behind the ears as you are."

Clay Allison didn't know whether he'd been insulted or simply joshed by the old-timer. He was about to decide he'd had enough of this old man.

"I know men who'd shoot you for saying something like that to 'em," the young man said in a serious tone.

"Now, you see what I mean, son? That's just what I'm talking about."

Clay Allison was once again confused and frowned at the older man.

"Why, when us old farts laugh at you young 'uns, it ain't you we're laughing at at all. It's the memory of how brash and full of vinegar and foolishness we were at your age. Don't you see?" he said as though the whole thing were as plain as day. And to Dallas Bodeen it likely was.

"Hmm. I'll have to think on that one."

"Well, while you do, just mount up and come with me," Dallas said, grabbing up the reins to his own horse. "I seen signs of wild turkey in this area. Maybe we can scare up a decent supper meal for the lot of us."

Clay Allison gathered up his own reins and remounted his horse, sore as he felt about the prospect. When he was in the saddle, he gave Dallas a glance and found a man with a serious look about him facing him.

"You know, son," Dallas said in a much quieter and sadder tone of voice, "sometimes those stories are all us old-timers have got left."

"I think I understand, Dallas," Clay Allison said with a short nod of the head. "I think I understand."

They traveled only three miles from where they planned on making camp, sure that they would be back before Will Carston and the rest would show up. And Dallas felt sure there might be a wild turkey or two down the trail. What they ran into was more than wild turkey.

They rode slowly toward a third horseman, as

though all three men were hunting the same prey. It was when the third rider got closer that Clay Allison suddenly found himself paying more attention to the ground than to the man riding toward them.

"That's one of them Wells Gang boys," he said in a low voice as he looked about for turkey sign on the far side of his mount. "I recognize him from the line shack."

"You got good eyes, son."

"Gotta be good at something, I reckon."

"Howdy, neighbor," Dallas said in his friendliest manner as the rider approached them. He only hoped the man wouldn't notice his Henry rifle, cocked and ready for use, conveniently stuck in the crook of his arm. After all, many a hunter was known to carry his weapon in such a manner. "Hunting supper, are you?"

The rider wasn't the cleanest shaven of men, but that wasn't uncommon on the trail. When water was scarce, a man would willingly go several days without touching a razor to his face.

"It would appear so," the rider said in his gruff voice. "Thought I seen sign of turkey hereabouts."

"Me too. Can't be far off, do you reckon?"

"Nope."

So far the conversation had gone well, but it was here that the rider started looking at Clay Allison in a strange way.

"Say, do I know you, mister?" he said, his voice turning a mite harder, a good deal more suspicious.

"I don't know, friend," Clay Allison said. "Could be." Dallas, sitting on his big horse, all but blocked the rider's view of young Allison.

"Ain't you the drunk came into that line shack a ways back?"

Clay shrugged. "Could be. That's where I come to, if you know what I mean." Clay leaned past Dallas a mite and grinned at the man, noticing he also had a rifle in the crook of his arm, likely ready to use.

"Say, wait a minute," the rider said, a sudden frown crossing his unshaven face. "The boss left word with Sam to take care of all of you."

It was right then that a turkey came gobbling and flirting about on the far side of Clay Allison's horse.

"I got supper!" he yelled. Then, in one quick motion, he pulled his six-gun and shot the gobbler's head off.

Whether the rider's intent was to try shooting the same turkey or to kill Dallas and Clay Allison, now that he had caught on to what was supposed to have taken place at the line shack, Dallas would never know. All he knew was that he didn't have to move the Henry rifle all that much from the crook of his arm to put a slug in the rider's chest and kill him dead before he even fell from his horse.

"So much for supper," Clay Allison said, holstering his six-gun as he took in the sight of what Dallas had done.

"This bird ain't going nowhere either" was all Dallas said.

"Wonder if he's got a price on his head?" Clay Allison dismounted, picked up the dead game, and tied it to his saddle.

"Won't find out till we get to Twin Rifles, I reckon. At least we'll have another horse among us."

"What about him?" Allison asked, motioning toward the dead man on the ground.

"Oh, I don't think he'll mind riding double with Sam," Dallas said with a straight face. "Never seen a corpse that had much to say about nothing anyway."

CHAPTER

★ 21 ★

It was pushing sundown by the time Pardee, Hank, Catherine, and me rode into camp that afternoon. Or maybe I should say evening.

"Are you sure this is the right camp?" Pardee asked, squinting at the grove in the distance.

"Why do you say that?" I asked. I had to squint a couple of times my own self before I could see what he was talking about. Or maybe we were simply too far off. Or maybe I was getting old. I had to admit that getting old was becoming a factor that weighed heavy on my mind the past few days. For a while that day I'd thought I was doing pretty good, not feeling lightheaded at all. But as the afternoon wore on and the heat hung there in the sky, I found myself tiring faster and faster. By the time that clump of cottonwoods came into sight and Pardee sighted the horses, why, I'd come to the determination that I wasn't about to try tracking these yahoos through the night. By God, I was in need of another good night's rest. And thank you, sir.

"Looks like three horses in camp," Pardee said. Then, looking over his shoulder at Hank, he added, "Dallas and that young Allison boy didn't take old Sam with 'em this morning, did they?"

Hank glanced down at his good arm and the reins he still held in his one good hand, the same reins he'd been holding damn near all day. "Nope," he said. "Old Sam's still as silent as ever. But I'll tell you what, Pardee. If they do have a third horse, I'll be almightly grateful for it. As far as we've come today, I've got a notion my ass and whatever it is I've been sitting on are about to become one. Nothing personal, you understand, son."

"Know what you mean, hoss," Pardee said. "Been feeling the same way my own self." Then, squinting at the cottonwoods and the horses next to the fire, he said, "By God, that *is* three mounts."

"Can you believe it?" Catherine said behind me. I thought her own voice was filled with a certain amount of amazement.

"Three horses? You bet your bonnet I can believe it, ma'am," I said. "Fact of the matter is, we could use another horse to boot."

"No, silly. Not the horses," she said. "I smell a turkey being cooked over that fire."

I took a long whiff of the air about me, and sure enough, she smelled a turkey being cooked.

"Well, I'll be damned, the woman's right," Hank said. There wasn't many a man or woman in this land who hadn't tasted turkey at one time or another in their lifetime. In fact, it was just a few years back that the government made the last Thursday of the month of November the official Thanksgiving Day. Of course, we'd been celebrating that particular day for some years long before the government ever took a hand in it.

I pulled the Colt Dallas had loaned me out of my holster and, hearing the sudden growl of my stomach, said, "Boys, I don't care whose camp that is down there. If they don't want to share some of that turkey I smell, I'm willing to fight 'em for a drumstick. Come on."

"Now you're talking," Pardee said and clicked his reins some, following me down toward the fire I could clearly see now.

"Took you long enough," Dallas said, stepping out of the shadows, his Henry rifle ready for a fight.

"Yeah, this old goat's been telling me we had to wait for our guests before I could dig into that bird," Clay Allison said, stepping out of the shadows, too. I thought I saw a crooked smile about him when he added, "I ain't much of a cook, but I figure that turkey's been done for close to half an hour now."

"Damn, boys, put the hardware away and get out the plates!" Hank said, climbing down from his saddle in a painful but grateful way. "You greeted us with the wrong implements, son, the wrong tools!"

Dallas took care to lean his Henry up against one of the cottonwoods, making sure it was handy in case there were unwelcome visitors to our camp. Not that I could blame him.

He brandished his trusty old bowie knife from a

well-worn sheath and said, "Now then, since I've got the biggest knife, I'll do the carving."

No one objected, not a whit, as Dallas did a masterful job of cutting through the bird and handing out portions to whoever was eating the dark and white meat.

At one point Catherine, who had so far taken in the whole procedure, decided to get her two bits' worth in. "I really have to thank you, Mr. . . . Dallas, is it?" she said in her politest manner.

"Actually, ma'am," Dallas said, pausing in his carving, "the kid over there is the one who got the supper." He nodded toward Clay Allison who was seated by one of the cottonwoods, viciously attacking a large drumstick. To me, Dallas smiled and said, *"I'm* the one who got you the extry horse."

"After you get through feeding your face, I hope you'll have time to tell me the story," I said. "Sounds like a humdinger."

"Believe me, Marshal, it is," Clay Allison said between bites. "It is." I thought I sensed a new kind of camaraderie between these two as the young gunman grinned at Dallas when he spoke.

I'm not even sure what part of that bird I ate that night, but it was tasty, mighty tasty. I hadn't had a bird so good since the last one Margaret Ferris cooked up a year back. All we needed was stuffing and berries and corn whatnot and that wouldn't have been a half bad meal. All we had was the bird and a cup of coffee that night, but it seemed to satisfy most of us.

I had to struggle to stay awake after the meal when Dallas and young Allison started talking about how they'd come on one of the Wells Gang and managed to kill him and the turkey at the same time.

"How far behind 'em do you think we are, Dallas?" I asked when he was through with his story.

"The way I figure it, ary they're settling down for the night, their horses needing a good rest as much as they do, I'd say five or six hours," Dallas said.

Five hours was a lot better than eight. Then again, it was a lot worse than only two or three. That meant we'd have to do some hard riding to finally catch up with that bunch. Hard riding I wasn't all that sure Pardee, Hank, and me were up to, truth be told. What was I going to do? Ask Dallas and that young buck Allison to go to Twin Rifles and fight off a gang of bank robbers at three-to-one odds? I'd be a fool to do that, nor would I ever be able to forgive myself. No, I'd have to make it to Twin Rifles one way or another and hope I could do my best to stop them from robbing the bank—again.

Still, what if I didn't make it? What if the Wells Gang managed to get to town before I did? What if they robbed the bank before I could get to them? The people of my town had risen up when they'd tried it the first time, running them out of town before they could even hold on to any money to run away with. Besides, Chance was the one I'd left in charge. He was a man of his own now, and he could do as good a job as I could in handling the Wells boys when they rode into town. But having Chance in my position worried me some. Like I said, Chance was the kind who would charge hell with a bucket of ice, put out the fire, and skate on the ice. But this was a well-armed gang of six my older son would be dealing with. What if he charged into them like I'd seen him do before and they cut him to shreds? What if they killed him? Killed my boy, Chance?

"How far ahead are they if they don't rest their horses, like they did last night?" I asked Dallas.

The old mountain man scratched his jaw as though thinking, then said, "Oh, five or six hours."

"What? But that's the same time as you said—"

"Better take it easy there, Will. I think that light-headedness is getting to you again," he said with that crooked smile of his.

"But—"

Dallas walked over to me and placed a firm hand on my shoulder.

"Listen, Will, I've got news for you. You've been riding today, but you ain't been keeping track of where you're going or what you've been doing," he said.

"Huh?" Maybe I was getting old and decrepit.

"Will, we ain't but a day or two out from Twin Rifles," Dallas said. "So the next day or so you best get as much rest as you can, because you're gonna need every ounce of strength in you, ary you want to be in on the fight with these bank robbers."

"Sounds to me like we oughta be turning in," Clay Allison said as he discarded one last meatless bone of that turkey.

No one argued the point.

No matter how close—or far away—we were from Bob Wells and his gang, one thing seemed evident. We weren't going to catch up with them until we were able to—that is, not until Pardee Taylor and Blacksnake Hank were able to ride harder and faster than the rest of us were now able to do. Me, I was getting better with each day, or at least that's what I thought. Maybe I wanted Wells and his gang so bad I was simply telling myself I was all right when I really wasn't. Maybe. All I knew was that I wanted that gang of bank robbers in the worst way. Or perhaps it was not wanting to fail the people of Twin Rifles, who had placed so much trust in me for so many years. If the two reasons weren't the same they were damn close to each other.

"I don't know," Dallas said with a grimace the next

morning as we finished our breakfast meal. Hank had brought up the subject of whether or not we'd get to Twin Rifles in time to stop the Wells Gang from robbing our bank. You'd have thought the whole thing pained Dallas, the way he was reacting to the question. And maybe it did. Who was to say? "You've got a point, Hank, but still . . ."

"Still, my ass!" the stagecoach driver said in what I reckon you could call a stubborn way. But then, that was Hank. "Begging your pardon, ma'am," he added with a tip of the hat.

By now I didn't expect to see either Catherine Innes or Blacksnake Hank come anywhere close to blushing. We'd all been through too much to worry about something as minor as a few cusswords.

"Of course I've got a point!" Hank said. "And as much as I'd like to kill off these bastards one by one my own self, the truth of the matter is that you folks are gonna make better time without dragging Pardee and me along."

"True," I said, tossing out the coffee grounds, "but the way I look at it, hoss, we're gonna need every gun and gun hand we can lay our hands on. Maybe you fellas can't ride too awful hard, but I know you're as full of fight as the rest of us and wanting to see these yahoos done in just as bad, although I know you each got your own reasons."

"Horse apples." Hank wasn't letting up on his stance, not one bit. "The way you talk about the folks in Twin Rifles, why, they'll come in right handy when this gang tries taking your town's money."

"True, but—"

Hank wasn't about to let me get a word in edgewise. "You know, you boys seem to be forgetting some-

151

thing," he said, speaking from the experience that comes with age. "This bank-robbery stuff is a new thing to most folks. Started in '66 with some bank back in Ohio, as I recollect. But these fellers that's too damn lazy to make a honest living, why, they're finding out the hard way that this ain't the easiest way of making a living at all."

"And how's that?" Dallas asked, not sure what the man was talking about.

"Why, the folks in your town are as good an example as any, I reckon," Hank said, the answer apparently as simple as pie to him. "Don't you see, it's those lads who've come back from the war. Those boys learned how to shoot and kill real well during that conflict, they did. They ain't gonna take no guff from anyone tries to have their way with 'em either, ary you get my drift."

I knew exactly what he was talking about, for my own younger son, Wash, was a prime example of it. Being on the losing side in any war ain't the easiest thing to come home to, so men like Wash were going to make sure that no one ever called them anything close to a coward. Fact of the matter was that at one time since they'd both returned, Wash had beaten the living tar out of his brother, and Chance is a mite bigger and maybe some tougher than Wash. Just goes to show what a good deal of determination can do for a body.

"That may be, Hank, but I'd still like to be there to open the ball when these pilgrims try robbing our bank again," I said with a certain amount of determination of my own. "The people in Twin Rifles may respond right well to an emergency, but the lot of us need to be there to sound that emergency for 'em.

Someone to put a hold on the Wells Gang so the rest of the folks can gather up their arms."

"What do you think, Clay?" Dallas asked young Allison, who had been relatively quiet about the whole subject until now.

Something changed in Clay Allison's disposition then, something I thought I'd seen in men before. I'd seen it on the face of both Chance and Wash when they'd nearly had their backs up against the wall and getting out alive was the only aim they had. Hell, maybe I'd had it on my own face at one time or another, I didn't know. But it was there on young Allison's face now as he spoke. "As long as it's self-defense, it don't matter to me who I kill," he said, an evil leer crossing his face as he spoke.

"That's good enough for me, son," Dallas said.

"Pardee, what do you say? You up to going it alone with Hank, or can you make it to Twin Rifles with us?" I asked, not at all sure what the lad's answer would be.

Pardee had been sitting there as quiet as a church mouse this morning, a pained look about him that I hadn't seen before. Maybe our riding, even as slow as it had been, was busting up his bones more than he cared to admit. Hell, he wouldn't be the first man— me among them—who said everything was all right when he knew good an' well he was feeling downright terrible. I reckon there's just one thing that makes a man feel as bad as being labeled a coward, and that's not being able to do his job when others are counting on him.

"I don't know, Will," he said in what sounded like a humble tone of voice. "I really want to go, but this side of mine—"

"Know what you mean, son," Hank said, interrupting him. He sure did seem to be doing an awful lot of that this morning. But in Pardee's case, he was likely saving face for the boy more than anything. "This arm of mine don't 'pear to be getting any better, either."

"I'm sorry, Will. I—"

"Don't worry about it, Pardee," I said, trying to sound as serious as I could, for the boy's sake. "You done fine so far. You'll make it."

"Well, that's what I been telling you, damn it!" It was Hank again, spouting off worse than I'd seen Old Faithful do. "With a rifle and a six-gun between us we can fend for ourselves. You folks need to get out of camp and catch up with those no good . . ." Then he stopped momentarily, likely remembering that he was in the presence of a woman.

"It's all right," Catherine said with a smile.

"You boys just do me a favor, if you will," Hank said.

"What's that?" I asked.

"Save at least one of 'em for me. I ain't about to let 'em get away with killing my horses. Not hardly!" I do believe everyone in camp knew he meant it, too.

"What about the woman?" Dallas asked now.

"What do you mean, what about the woman?" This came from a rather determined Catherine Innes, by the sound of her voice. "Why, I'm going, of course!"

I reckon most of us men had been in enough arguments with a woman at one time or another to know that winning one was out of the question.

So that was that as we broke camp and prepared to go after the Wells Gang in earnest.

CHAPTER
★ 23 ★

Rachel sick today, Miss Margaret?" Chance asked as Margaret Ferris poured him a cup of coffee and prepared to take his order. It was after the regular noon lunch hour, and Chance had already had a beer at Ernie Johnson's saloon, preparatory to eating his midday dinner at the Ferris House. When he was in town, and when he could afford it, he enjoyed taking his meals at the Ferris House for at least the sight and company of Rachel Ferris, Margaret's attractive young daughter, if not for the tasty meals his father bragged about. But for the last day or two he was waited on by Margaret, Rachel having been nowhere in sight when he had arrived. So he determined to ask whether the woman he had taken a liking to was indeed sick.

"Actually, Chance, I believe she's avoiding you," Margaret said in what Chance thought to be that above-it-all way she could have about her sometimes.

"Avoiding me!" Chance said in total astonishment. "What for? What did I do to her to deserve that?" He found himself getting mad at the thought of being put off like this.

"I believe it has something to do with a comment you made about the gentler sex," she said with raised eyebrow. "In fact, considering the source, you might count yourself lucky to be waited on at all in this establishment, *Mister* Carston."

Chance glared at the woman taking his order. He found himself confused about the whole affair. "What the devil are you talking about, lady?" Two could play at this game, he decided, trying to be just civil enough so he could get a meal out of Margaret Ferris. After all, there was just so much a man could take when you came down to it. Especially when you considered how empty your stomach was feeling at the time. "Just pan-fry me whatever meat is your specialty today," he quickly added, making sure he at least got his order in before being physically thrown out of the place. And he knew Margaret Ferris could do it, too. All she needed was an iron skillet in her hand and that woman could have her way with any man on earth.

"I imagine she can explain that to you when she's good and ready," Margaret said in a stern manner. "The source, by the way, was that young upstart, Pardee Taylor. I can't say as he knows much when it comes to being discreet." Then she stomped off, her head stuck up in the air, giving anyone looking her way an impression of the proud woman Margaret Ferris truly was.

"I'm gonna have to talk to that boy," Chance mumbled under his breath.

In fifteen minutes Margaret was back, balancing two plates on one arm as she held the coffee pot in her other hand. She still seemed a bit perturbed at Chance for what he had done, although Chance still wasn't sure what it was he'd said that was so bad. Once Margaret had placed the steak before him and a plate of home-fried potatoes beside him and refilled his coffee cup, she set down the coffee pot and folded her arms.

"By the way, young man, just how do you plan on paying for this meal?" she asked.

Chance wasn't going to tell her, but in the stance she had struck, Margaret Ferris reminded him an awful lot of his own mother when she was a mite mad at him for his foolhardiness during his younger years. Something to do with vanity and age, he recalled Pa saying to him at some point a year or two back.

"Well, Pa's got me sitting in for him while he's gone," Chance said, cutting his meat into smaller chunks. "I thought maybe the city council would pay for my meals, too, just like Pa's."

"Not on your life, Chance Carston," Margaret said in a huff.

"But—"

"The city council will pay for the amount of food Will Carston eats, but not the amount of food *you* put away. Why, you'd eat me out of business in a week if I operated that way!"

Chance shrugged, knowing he couldn't win any kind of battle with this woman.

"I'm open to suggestions," he said as he stuffed another piece of meat in his mouth.

"That being the case, you get out around this area and see if you can't round me up some more deadwood for firewood," she said, her voice ringing with authority. "I only got about two or three days' worth of firewood out of that young Taylor boy and that old man your father seems to like, Dallas."

"Yes, ma'am."

"Well, I need to have some more deadwood gathered before I can have it chopped, so that's what I want you to do before you'll get your meal tomorrow afternoon. No later than two o'clock, understand?" She could have been a stern schoolteacher giving out assignments, if the tone of her voice was any indication.

"Yes, ma'am."

"I want to have enough wood for Will to chop once he gets back," she added. Then all the toughness seemed to leave her, as though the mention of Will Carston's name could do that to her, which Chance knew to be the truth. "If he comes back," she said in a soft, sad voice.

"Sit down, Margaret. I don't want you fainting on my food," Chance said, pushing his nearly empty plate of food aside. When Margaret did as Chance said, he gulped the last of his coffee, refilled his cup, and said, "Worry a lot about him, do you?"

Trying to regain some of her composure, Margaret pulled a kerchief from out of nowhere and dabbed at the corner of her eye. "Yes, I suppose I do worry about him more than I should."

Chance nodded. "He's been a grown man for some years now," he said. "I know he's taken every chance he could to remind me and Wash of it over the years. I don't think you'll find much on this earth that'll keep Pa from doing what he sees fit. No, ma'am."

Margaret sniffed back what Chance thought to be tears before saying, "Oh, I know it's probably needless worry, but I can't seem to help myself. Not this time."

"How come? I don't understand." If Chance sounded confused about her reasoning, perhaps it was because he was indeed confused about the species called women and how they thought. All he could remember his pa saying was that they were wily as foxes and twice as tricky in their thinking.

"Well, this time he's alone. Don't you see, Chance, this time you and Wash aren't with him," she said, bringing a voice of logic to her thought. "Before, when you boys went out, you always went with one or the other, or all three of you went out. But this time," she said, her voice sounding smaller now, "well, Will's alone."

"Let me tell you something, Margaret," Chance said, taking one of her small hands in his big hamlike fist, as though such an action would comfort her. "Pa was out on his own long before he got hitched to Ma so long ago. And even when he did get hitched and way before us boys come into this world, why, he was out in the wilderness providing for Ma. He did it all by himself, Margaret, and he'll keep on doing it that way until there ain't no more outlaws to chase on this frontier. Hell, I figure he takes us boys along on those adventures of his just to have someone to give a hard time to," Chance added as an afterthought.

His words seemed to do Margaret Ferris some good, bolster her spirits. The smile on her face wasn't what you'd call forced, but Chance thought he'd seen her on happier days.

"You're probably right, Chance. I'm probably just worrying for nothing," she admitted, her smile broadening.

"You know what Pa says about worrying, don't you?"

"Yes," she said, and this time Chance knew the smile on her face was genuine. He knew she had reached back in time to come up with the memory that had entered her being, as she said, "As I recall, he told me long ago that worrying was a lot like riding a rocking horse. 'It'll keep you busy, but you won't get a damn thing done,' he said."

"That's it," Chance said with a grin, as though authenticating what she'd said.

"Haven't you wondered what's happened to Pardee Taylor and that old-timer, Dallas?" Margaret said when Chance forked the last piece of his meat into his mouth and took to chewing it, sipping more coffee in between.

"Well, Margaret, I've got to admit to wondering just what in the deuce happened to those two," he said once he finished swallowing his food. "I just sent Pardee out to deliver those papers and told him to get right back here." Here he shrugged. "Maybe Dallas met him on the way out. He was gonna track down that coach and see what was going on. Could be the two of 'em met up and found a bottle between 'em. They've both been known to put away some Taos Lightning, you know."

"I know, but it wouldn't seem that a bottle of whiskey would last that long between those two," she said. "In fact, I would suspect a hangover would last longer than the bottle of whiskey."

"You've got a point, Margaret. You've got a point."

"Do you intend on doing anything about it?"

Chance thought a minute, finishing off his coffee, before answering. "I'll round up that deadwood you're needing tomorrow, Miss Margaret, and if they haven't returned to Twin Rifles by sundown, why, I do believe I'll start a little expedition of my own the next day."

"Thanks, Chance," Margaret said, and this time it was she who took the big man's hand in her own. "You've put my mind at ease."

"I sure do wish Rachel would put my mind at ease with this avoiding she's doing of me," he said as he got up and put on his hat. "It purely puzzles me, Margaret. I mean to tell you, it purely does for a fact."

Margaret smiled at Chance. "I'll tell you what. I'll talk to Rachel tonight about it. Maybe I can calm her down and she'll be able to talk to you about this whole situation tomorrow when you're eating your noon meal."

There was hope in Chance's eyes, hope in his face, as he pumped her hand. "I'd really appreciate it, Margaret. Come to think of it, I seen a couple of big pieces of deadwood down by the creek a mile or so out of town. Might be able to drag 'em on back for you. Yes, ma'am."

"And remember what I said, Chance," she said as he made his way to the door of the Ferris House. "No later than two o'clock."

"Yes, ma'am," Chance said, tipping his hat to her, "no later than two o'clock. Yes, ma'am."

CHAPTER
★ 24 ★

In a way it felt strange, riding my horse as fast as I was, particularly after I'd been doing nothing but plodding along for the last few days. But like I said I was feeling a mite better and thought I could make a good distance that day.

Tracking the Wells Gang wasn't all that hard, either. Like Dallas had pointed out more than once along the way, they didn't seem too worried about leaving a trail, likely because they had originally thought there wouldn't be anyone to follow them back to Twin Rifles. They didn't know how wrong they were, the fools, I thought to myself as we rode along. If we stuck to the trail they were leaving and did our best to track them down, why, we might even be there to greet them when they tried robbing our bank again. That was what I kept telling myself, what I kept running through the back of my mind. But it wasn't the only thing.

Even more than catching up with these killers and thieves was the thought of leaving a couple of good men like Pardee Taylor and Blacksnake Hank back there as we'd broken camp this morning. Still, Hank had insisted that he and Pardee could make their way to Twin Rifles by themselves and do it without our help. Both men were pretty busted up and had a right to be complaining as much as anyone, but they weren't. Not about being taken care of, anyway.

At least Hank seemed to realize and understand that, wounded or not, for me catching Bob Wells was my first priority. After all, he was the one I was initially transporting to the law at Fort Dodge. He'd escaped, with the help of his gang, and when I caught up with him now, well, there would just be a few more charges filed against him by the time I got him to Fort Dodge. Hell, if they didn't hang Bob Wells for those murders he was wanted for up Kansas way, why, I'd hang the man my own self. I was that mad at him.

"Got something on your mind, Will?" Dallas asked when we made a dry camp at noon for a short period of time. By then I had a notion we were getting closer to Twin Rifles, for some of the territory I was seeing in the distance was looking familiar to me now. We'd covered a lot of flat land, just as I remembered from the stagecoach ride up the trail. We had also come on occasional pieces of woodland, which was where most of the small streams and water holes were located. And in the distance—off to the west, I gauged—I thought I saw the fringe of what was a small mountain range. Oh, yes, we were getting closer and closer to Twin Rifles, of that I was sure.

I shrugged. I reckon what I was thinking showed more than I had thought. "I reckon I'm just having second thoughts about the way we left Pardee and Hank back there," I said, tossing a thumb over my shoulder.

"Yes," Catherine said, a guilty look about her, "I feel the same way. Those poor men really need someone to look after them. Really."

"Now, that may be, lady," Clay Allison said around a chew of hardtack, "but the way I see it, you had your chance to stay with 'em and help 'em out. You give that up when you made such a fuss about going along with us." He didn't say it outright, but I got the distinct notion that young Clay Allison wasn't too keen on having a woman along on our trek to Twin Rifles. I found myself wondering if he was the kind of man who was just too polite to say so. He wouldn't be the first, you know.

"Oh, I wouldn't worry about 'em," Dallas said with a crooked smile, apparently not worried about the two at all. "That old bullwhacker strikes me as the kind who'd feed a rattler his own venom and watch it die just so's he could make a meal out of it. And if a rattlesnake don't bother him, why, I reckon he can look after himself and that Pardee Taylor, too, if need be."

"Reminds you of your own self, I'll bet," I said. I'd known Dallas Bodeen for thirty-some years, maybe forty. I didn't think I could remember back that far. But I'd come to know the man well over those years

164

and could easily tell when he was funning with and about others.

That same crooked smile quickly appeared on Dallas's face again as he replied, "Now that you mention it, he does remind me of my own self."

"Must be his age," Clay Allison said with his own version of a crooked grin. Knowing that Dallas was as touchy as me about his age, I was surprised he let the kid get away with that kind of a smart-alecky comment.

"Just wait until you get to be as wordly as these two gentlemen," Catherine said in what I took to be a tactful way of calling us old duffers without calling us old duffers. If you follow my line of thought.

"I can hardly wait," the young gunman said with a shake of disbelief to his head. "What say we move out?" He tossed out the remains of a cup of water and headed for his horse.

"Sounds good to me," Dallas said and did the same.

Me, I helped Catherine to her feet, doing what I thought came naturally to a man—helping a woman out and all, you know. But she surprised me when she came into my arms and landed a whale of a kiss on my lips, a kiss hard enough to knock me down as fast as any bullet. Like all of her kisses, it left me stuttering and stammering for the right words and afraid to speak them when I found them. This time, as infatuated with this woman as I felt at times, I decided it was time to square the books on this account once and for all.

"That was a right fine kiss, Miss Catherine," I said, taking hold of her shoulders as I pushed her away from me. "It really was."

"I know" was all she said in reply, adding that catlike smile a wily woman will make at times. "I meant it to be."

I didn't really want to admit it, to myself or anyone else, but with all the thinking on capturing Bob Wells and his gang and pondering on whether we should or should not have left Pardee and Hank back there . . . well, the subject of Catherine Innes and her notions toward me was also weighing heavy on my mind.

"Miss Catherine, there's something you've got to know and know for sure." I'd rather have fought old Santy Ana and his army back when Texas was still young than have to face this woman and tell her what I had to tell her. I'll be the first one to admit, you know, that in a situation like this words ain't exactly my long suit.

"Oh?" If the look on her face was any indication, she knew something was about to go awry between us. And it was me who was going to do it.

"Yes, ma'am." I hemmed and hawed, searching for the right words. "You're gonna have to stop this kissing business."

"Why? I thought you liked it. You didn't seem to have any qualms about it when I was saving your life just after that stagecoach fiasco." If this woman was a schoolteacher, she was all of a sudden acting like a real high-minded one. Know-it-all like, you understand.

"Yes, ma'am, and I appreciate it. But it's got to stop. You ain't my woman, no matter what you may be thinking." I had to get it all out, had to make her sure she knew where I stood on this matter, so what came out of my mouth next surprised me as much as it did Catherine Innes, Dallas, and young Allison, the last two making no pretense about not listening in on our conversation. They had their ears stuck out like some town gossip, which was close to the truth in Dallas's case. "Truth of the matter is, ary I've got a woman, why, I'd have to say it's Margaret Ferris," I said.

I could have slapped Catherine across the face and she couldn't have been more surprised. "The older woman at the Ferris House who served us during the stage stop," she said, more as though stating a fact than asking a question.

"Yes, ma'am. That's a fact," I said, suddenly realizing that I was likely just as embarrassed about this whole thing as she was. An abrupt flush came to my cheeks, and I felt as though I'd been facing the sun for a good hour straight, my face felt that hot.

"Well, I'm happy for you." Catherine Innes was crestfallen to say the least, her voice now barely audible. Maybe she really was in love with me, but I found that hard to believe. A man my age and a woman her age? It just didn't make any kind of sense. "I'm happy for her."

"Miss Margaret?" Dallas said in a tone that wasn't shock so much as wanting to know for sure if what I'd said was really the truth. After all, I could have been lying just to get the woman off my back, although there are some who would argue that point I'm sure.

"Dallas, mount up," I growled at the man.

"Come on, old-timer," Clay Allison said, gently taking hold of Dallas's elbow and leading him toward our horses. "That's killing meanness in his voice, if I'm any judge."

When they were out of earshot, I turned back to

Catherine, my grip now gone from her shoulders. Instead, I'd dropped my hands to my sides in what I'm sure was a useless-looking manner.

"Darlin', as long as I've walked this earth, there are at least two things I've learned," I said softly. "You can't force a man to love you, and you can't stop all the death and destruction that takes place on this earth. It's just too much to ask of anyone." There was silence between us as I saw the tears well up in her eyes, wishing I could do something to stop them, knowing that what I had to say next would only bust open the dam. "You're a fine-looking young lady, Catherine, but I'm not in love with you, never have been and never will be. So what you think we got between us has got to stop now. Understand?"

By then she was in tears and that hanky of hers had appeared out of nowhere and she was dabbing at her eyes. After a couple of minutes the well sort of dried up some, and she was able to mount her horse again.

"Margaret Ferris, huh?" Dallas said, testing the limits of my patience again.

On my horse, I said through gritted teeth, "Dallas, ary you don't keep your mouth shut, there's gonna be one less ex-Ranger in this world, and he'll likely be the one I ride into Twin Rifles with, draped over his saddle."

Dallas Bodeen shut his mouth. I reckon he knew I meant business.

CHAPTER
★ 25 ★

Catherine Innes was silent the rest of the day. We did what I might not otherwise have considered some moderately hard riding, for I could remember days when we'd ridden a hell of a lot harder than today. I reckon that head wound was still bothering me a mite and it was just the notion I'd set in my mind that was telling me I was doing fine. Maybe.

As easy as the trail was to follow, we still hadn't caught up with Bob Wells and his boys by the time we came on a water hole and a small grove of trees and decided to call it quits for the day. Dallas and young Clay Allison said it was because the horses were getting worn out and tired, but I had my own suspicions that they had been taking in my own declining performance that afternoon when they decided to make camp. I would have been hard pressed to admit it to anyone else, much less my own self, but by the end of the day I felt a good deal of my energy had been sapped from me. And I couldn't prove it, but I had a sneaking suspicion that those two would have forged on and tried to overtake the Wells Gang, be it daylight or dark. But they were saddled with me and a woman, so they were taking their time, apparently confident that we'd catch up with the killers calling themselves the Wells Gang soon enough.

We were running low on coffee, but Dallas seemed to think that tomorrow we'd make it to Twin Rifles, so he made a good strong pot of the black stuff, leaving enough for one more pot tomorrow morning. After young Allison gathered up some firewood for her, Catherine silently went about fixing up some supper with what little foodstuffs Dallas had left in his pack. Me, I hoped these two—Catherine and young Allison—weren't going to take a liking to each other like that which had taken place between Catherine and me. I wasn't sure I could stand to see anything like that again.

I reckon what I did most once we'd made camp was sit there and think. Not that it was what I did best so much as the fact that I had a lot of time to do nothing more than think. Besides, I'd been mulling over a question or two in my mind that afternoon, knowing that Dallas and Clay Allison were keeping their eyes on the trail we were following and needed precious little assistance from me. Truth be known, at times I thought I'd just been brought along as some type of symbol of law and order more than an active lawman looking for an escaped murderer and bank robber.

After all, I was the only one wearing a lawman's badge.

"Still thinking, are you, Will?" Dallas said halfway through our evening meal. To young Allison he added, "Will's real good at sizing things up, you know. Real good." If that was supposed to sound like a compliment, I wasn't in the mood for it, knowing full well it was likely my old pard's lame attempt to get back on my good side. Dallas was like that. I knew, for I'd seen him act this way toward Cora years ago. Him and Cora had fought like cats and dogs when the chance arose. Lord, could they fight.

"As a matter of fact I am, Dallas," I said around a mouthful of beans. "I've had a burr under my saddle for the better part of the afternoon."

"I've always found that the thing about having a burr under your saddle is it's the horse that gets bothered most by it," Dallas said in what I suppose was a philosophical tone for him. "Just what is it that's bothering you, Will?"

"Actually, it's what *should* be bothering *you,* Dallas," I said. "As long as you were with the Rangers, I'd think it would be bothering you."

This seemed to embarrass the man some, for he soon had young Allison looking at him with a frown, as though he had overlooked something the young gunman knew nothing about. If that was indeed true, Clay Allison would soon be checking the loads of his pistol, of that I was sure.

"Oh? And just what is it I should be wary of, old hoss?" Dallas still hadn't caught on to what I was getting at. Maybe we were both getting old, for I had chastised myself this afternoon for not thinking of it sooner. I knew that if I came across the wrong answers, why, it could wind up getting us killed.

I poured the last of the coffee between us and set the pot aside, watching the fire fade away as the sun did the same for that day.

"You remember telling me how you come on that extra horse we got?" I said.

"Sure," Clay said. "That was the afternoon me and Dallas rode out ahead of you all and wound up with a turkey and a rattler all in one afternoon."

I couldn't remember ever talking sassy like that when I was young. Or maybe I did spout off like young Allison did and I didn't remember. One thing I knew now was that I didn't like it all that much. But then, that's what comes with age, I reckon.

"That's a fact," Dallas said, confirming Clay Allison's remark.

"Maybe I'm getting old, Dallas, but didn't you figure someone else from the Wells Gang would come back a-looking for that yahoo once they found he was missing? Or am I missing something here?" Hell, maybe Dallas had mentioned it to me and I just hadn't remembered what he'd said. Maybe I was indeed getting old.

"Well, it's like this, Will," my friend said, gulping down the last of his lukewarm coffee and tossing out the remains. "I only had that one run-in with the fella at the cabin, and when I got through, why, he wasn't doing much palavering at all, if you recall."

"Yeah."

"But from hearing you folks talk about these outlaws, that old stage driver and young Pardee Taylor included, why, I got to figuring that they're as shiftless and untrustworthy as most of those pilgrims we had to deal with in the old days. You know, run together like a pack of wolves long as it suits their purposes but would kill one another if the chips were down. Heathens like that, you understand."

"I follow you so far."

Dallas shrugged. "I told the kid here that I thought the rest of the gang would figure the fella we killed quit the bunch and took off on his own. You know, heading for Old Mexico or some such. It wouldn't be the first time it had happened, you know."

"I don't doubt that, friend," I said, feeling a good deal of worry within me now. "But what if they *did* send someone back to track that feller they sent out first off? What if they did send him back and—"

"Then you'd be in a mighty bad situation." I heard the words at the same time I saw Clay Allison going for his six-gun, about to pull it out of his holster like the distrusting person I was figuring him to be when news like this got out. But he only got as far as putting his hand on the butt of his pistol. He froze solid as a rock when he saw the hombre step out from behind one of the trees in that grove. He had a gun in his own hand and looked mean enough to use it without making any speeches or caring to hear any reasons why you did or didn't do what he said. "You touch that gun, sonny, and I'll kill you here and now." I'd heard similar words from Pardee Taylor only a week or so back, and they sounded just as deadly when spoken by this tough. Maybe more so.

"I'd do what he says, kid," I said with a mite of caution. It was then I noticed that Catherine was suddenly clinging to my side, a look of terror in her eyes. Until that time we'd been sitting a few feet apart as we ate, but now she was sticking to the side of me like I was the only person who could save her from this man. And who's to say, maybe I was. In a softer voice I said to her, "It's all right, darlin', we'll be all right." I wasn't sure how true those words were, but I couldn't tell her we were going to be dead before the night was out, now, could I?

"Damn," I heard Dallas mutter under his breath. No one likes to admit to being wrong, but this time Dallas had staked our lives on maybe being wrong, and at the moment it was looking like a fatal mistake indeed.

I didn't know what this fellow's name was, and he didn't say. Fact of the matter is, he had it set in his mind what he was going to do to us, and no discussing the matter was needed. "Old man, I see some rope on that bay over there," he said to Dallas after instructing us all to drop our weapons. "You fetch it real careful like and cut me about six three-foot lengths. Then you toss that bowie of yours over on the pile of guns. Understand?"

"Sure. You just take it easy, mister," Dallas said in a tamer tone now. "Ain't no reason to get pushy about it."

"You make one false move and I'll start killing people," the outlaw growled, a harsh look coming to his face that was nearly as mean as the way he spoke. "And I'll start with the cute one here," he added, presently shifting his six-gun's point of aim to Catherine Innes. Even with the black eye and the darkish bruise on her cheek, Catherine was still a mighty pretty lady.

At first I couldn't figure out why he wanted six pieces of rope. It seemed obvious that he would tie each of us up by hand and foot, but my knowledge of numbers told me that was only enough rope for three of us. What crossed my mind next was a horrible thought, but it turned out to be just what the man had in mind. The three that he tied up were Dallas, Clay Allison, and me. It was when the man ran out of rope that Catherine figured out he was going to have his way with her, at least if the shudder I saw her give off was any indication.

"No, please," she said in a voice that was only a whisper, fear having taken over her feelings. "You can't do this. Please . . ." She backed up against one of the trees before being stopped as the outlaw continued to approach her, a leer on his face.

It was then I heard a horse approaching camp. It was traveling at what you might call a slow lope, if there is such a thing. If only for the moment, it gave Catherine Innes a reprieve as the outlaw frowned and backed into the shadows.

"Don't nobody say nothing or I'll kill the lot of you outright, got it?" he said in a low voice that was dead serious in intent.

Dallas, young Allison, and me nodded silently that we understood. Catherine was too scared to say or do anything.

I should have known it was Pardee Taylor without even having to see him first. He'd been walking into situations like this on a real steady basis for a week or two now. First there was that bank robbery back in Twin Rifles, when he got stuck in between a handful of these yahoos. Then there was the relay station and—

"Evening fellas," he said jovially as he sauntered into camp, his rifle hanging at his side, looking as though nothing was wrong in his world. He was smiling as he said, "Didn't think I'd make it this far, busted up and all, did you?" Then he took in the fact that except for Catherine we were all seated, our hands behind our backs, our feet visibly tied together, our guns in a pile on the far side of the camp. Then, like some dumb oaf, he said, "Say, what's wrong here? What's—"

The outlaw suddenly appeared, his own six-gun still in hand. "What's wrong is you walked in on something you shouldn't have. Now I'll have to kill you, too."

The strangest thing happened then. If Pardee Taylor was indeed some sort of buffoon, he sure didn't act like it. He had this sly-looking grin on his face as he said, "Is that so?" It must have been some more foolishness he'd learned from Chance and those crazy stories my son was telling him. Whatever it was, it threw the outlaw as much as it did me, for he frowned at Pardee in what I gauged to be a good deal of confusion.

"What did you say?" the man asked.

I don't know what Pardee's answer would have been, but he never had to make it. Quick as you please a knife flew over his shoulder from somewhere behind, and landed square in the middle of the outlaw's chest. His eyes got big with surprise as he stared in amazement at Pardee. But he must have thought he'd try killing Pardee before he died his own self. He cocked his six-gun as he took one step forward. He never did make it, though, for Pardee Taylor had also taken a stride forward to meet him, and his big hand grasped the outlaw's revolver as the man tried to pull the trigger. Pardee yanked the gun from his fist, the only thing keeping it from going off being his thumb, which he'd stuck between the hammer and the cylinder. Our outlaw friend fell to the ground next to the fading fire, nearly as dead as the embers of that fire. I reckon what did him in was the force of his body falling on that knife. I heard him make one final gasp before he was dead.

"Fooled you, didn't I?" Pardee said with a smile, laying his rifle down and starting to cut my bonds.

"That you did, son," I started to say. "But how—"

"Forgot I even existed, didn't you?" Blacksnake Hank said in his old cantankerous way, stepping out of the shadows, a six-gun in his one good hand. "Still got one good arm, you know." I'd completely forgotten the stagecoach driver and the fact that he'd been traveling double saddle with Pardee. I reckon I am getting old.

"You come in right handy, old-timer," Clay Allison said to the man behind him as Pardee cut his bonds. But he was looking at Dallas when he spoke, and I had the notion there was some kind of special meaning going on between these two men that I didn't know the first thing about. Some friendships have the strangest bonds a body can imagine.

"I wondered if anyone would ever get around to saying that," Hank said with a scowl. Which was when Catherine walked over to him and kissed him gently on the cheek. If that woman wasn't careful, she'd have a reputation as being something other than a schoolteacher. But for the moment that kiss perked Hank right up.

"I wonder if we'll have any more unfriendly visitors tonight," Clay Allison said as he picked up and holstered his own six-gun and proceeded to disperse the rest among us.

"I don't think so," I said as I holstered my gun. "It

took Wells a couple of days to come to the decision that something was wrong with the first man he'd sent after us."

"Hell, yes," Dallas said, catching on to my train of thought. "That Wells character, why, he don't know how far back these compadres of his had to go, or if they went at all. Like I said, this is a shiftless bunch you're dealing with. And none too trustworthy among themselves."

"You boys think they're more concerned with the money in your bank than anything else, is that it?" young Allison asked.

"That's it." I nodded.

"Me and Dallas will take a turn at guard tonight," Clay Allison volunteered. "The rest of you folks better turn in for the night." At times Clay Allison could be a real gentleman about things.

Catherine scraped together some food for Hank and Pardee, who hadn't eaten yet. It was while they were eating that I got curious.

"Just what made you two ride hard enough to catch up with us?" I asked, knowing they must have been feeling a good deal of discomfort if not pain by now, although I had yet to hear either of them complain about it.

"Me and young Pardee here, we got to talking amongst ourselves," Hank said between bites of food. "Hell, it was that or talk to the horse. Anyway, we decided you folks might be able to use an extra hand after all."

"Well, it's a good thing you did what you did," I said, hoping they knew how grateful I felt toward them.

"Wouldn't miss this run-in with the Wells Gang for

the world," Pardee said with what I thought to be a genuine grin.

"Well, you won't have long to wait, son," I said. "I figure tomorrow we'll be in Twin Rifles."

And so would the Wells Gang. I didn't have to say any more, knowing the same thought was running through every one else's mind, too.

CHAPTER

★ 26 ★

Breakfast the next morning was a quiet affair, although no one complained about the lack of conversation. We all knew we'd be arriving in Twin Rifles sometime today, all depending on how fast we lit out after the Wells Gang. I didn't know if that silence was an omen of death, nor did I know what was going through the minds of the others in our group, but there was a growing tension in the air as the day began, and I didn't particularly like it.

Dallas made the rest of the coffee, and Catherine fried the few pieces of bacon left in Dallas's possibles sack. No one made a fuss about using up the rest of our supplies, for we all knew we'd either be able to get a decent meal at the Ferris House or the Porter

Café . . . or we'd be dead, in which case food wouldn't matter worth a damn anyway.

It was a relief to know that when we broke camp each of us would have a horse to ride. The member of the Wells Gang who had tried to do us in didn't have an awful lot to say about things and wound up riding double with Sam, the other gang member Dallas had killed a few days back. I didn't think he'd mind the company, and Hank didn't seem to mind leading that load along as we set out to capture Bob Wells and his gang. Or die trying.

I still had Catherine's makeshift bandage wrapped around my forehead. She'd taken time the night before to pull me off to the side of the dying fire and change it one last time, applying a fresh piece of wrapping to it and assuring me that it would be fine until we got to Twin Rifles. I reckon there's something about a fresh bandage on a wound that gives a body confidence in survival. Or maybe it's the words of the one doing the bandaging, telling you that you are going to be just fine, that help. Whatever it is, I felt a lot better that morning, confident in some manner that I would be able to give the Wells boys a run for their money and maybe even survive the encounter. The only thing that stuck in my craw that morning was Catherine's final words to me just before leaving for the far side of the camp to make her bed for the night.

"I'm sorry it couldn't have worked out differently for us, Will," she'd said in a sad way. "I really am." But she didn't give me a chance to respond to her words before she made a quick exit of the area. Me, I sensed that this wasn't the time to discuss such matters. Hell, maybe it would never be the time to discuss what she thought went on between us. So I let it go at that and went to sleep, telling myself that I'd talk to her once this bank-robbing matter was taken care of.

We didn't ride out hell-for-leather, as you might expect. Oh, it was important to get to Twin Rifles and stop the Wells Gang from trying to rob our bank again, but we all knew we'd need every available gun we could muster to do it. And I knew that if it came down to it, the people of Twin Rifles could hold their own against this gang, at least until we got there. And I don't mind telling you that having Pardee Taylor and Blacksnake Hank along made me feel a whole lot better about taking on those yahoos. So we took off at a friendly sort of lope, Dallas and Clay Allison and Catherine and me knowing that a slow pace would be a lot easier on Pardee and Hank as they tried to keep up with us.

I didn't know what good Catherine Innes would be once we got there, but I did know that both Pardee and Hank were more than willing to fight these outlaws we were chasing. They'd said so the night before, and I had no reason to doubt their word on the subject. Hell, you don't wander into a camp knowing there's likely a man in there who could kill you on the spot if he took the notion without having some kind of guts, and that was just what Pardee had done. As we rode on, I made a mental note to tell Pardee he was doing a fine job. Everybody needs to be told they're doing a good job every once in a while, and Pardee Taylor, for all his trying, seemed long overdue for a pat on the back. Lord knows the people of Twin Rifles had been giving him a kick in the ass long enough.

The hours wore on and the sun was out and hot as

could be, but somehow I didn't mind it that much, for even with my oversized buckskin jacket I'd noticed a good chill in the air the night before. The cold night air had made the sun a welcome sight to me and, I was sure, the rest of us as we rode on that morning. I'd heard stories about the Indians and how many of the tribes believed that the sun had great healing powers, and who was to say, perhaps there was some truth to that. I know that as we followed the trail of the Wells Gang, I could feel the warmth of the sun on my body and found myself feeling a new surge of energy within me. The more we rode, the stronger I felt. Maybe there was something to those Indian stories about Old Sol. Or maybe I was simply fooling myself with false confidence as we rode to our showdown with this outlaw gang. I did my best to put that thought out of my mind, knowing that this was one time when dwelling on something too much was not a good thing.

As flat as much of the land had been, we were soon upon the creek and wooded land that sprouted up for a mile or two north of Twin Rifles. Wells and his men had crossed this creek, but as soon as we did the same, Dallas, who was leading our expedition, came to a sudden halt.

"What's the matter, hoss?" I asked, pulling up beside him.

"I don't know, Will," he said, scratching his head in apparent puzzlement. "Looks like they decided to split up here and go their separate ways." He indicated the tracks before us, which suggested the Wells Gang had indeed split up, half going off to the left, half off to the right of Twin Rifles.

"Can't blame 'em, can you?" Clay Allison said.

"How's that?" Pardee asked.

"Well, they've been in this town before and tried robbing your bank before, right?"

"Yeah." Pardee nodded, apparently catching on to the young gunman's train of thought. "I see what you mean. They're known men now."

"Hell, yes!" Allison said with emphasis. "I'll tell you something, friend. I damn sure wouldn't want to ride into a town and get shot out of the saddle before I could rob the bank. You can bet on that."

"But what if they did ride on?" Dallas apparently wasn't convinced of Allison's theory. "Remember what I said about these rattlesnakes. They're shiftless as can be and likely lacking in guts when it comes to doing something individually. I'm wondering if, after that last reception they got, some of these boys hadn't developed a bad case of jaundice about the belly area and backs of their bodies."

"You think they're sick?" Catherine asked in bewilderment.

"Not quite, Miss Catherine," Hank said. Like the rest of us, Hank knew that jaundice was a yellowing of the skin, which was what Catherine Innes must have initially thought. "What Dallas is describing, ma'am, borders more on cowardice than any kind of sickly feeling you might attach to a man."

"I see."

"Could be they snuck around back of the bank and whatever building is across the street from it," Clay Allison said. "That's what I'd do."

"Say, just what is your profession anyway, son?" Dallas asked, a serious frown crossing his face. "I mean, you're talking an awful lot like one of them bank robbers."

Young Allison held up a hand as though to ward off

a blow from the old mountain man talking to him. With a grin, he said, "I'm a cattleman, honest." When his humor seemed wasted on Dallas, he added, "Hey, I'm just trying to think like one of those fellas would ponder it. Isn't that what you'd do?"

"You've got a point, son, you've got a point," I said, admitting that he was right. You don't get to be successful at hunting deer by thinking like a fish or a bird. Oh, they've all got places they can escape to, but they're different places with different escape routes. I thought for a moment before saying, "I think young Clay has the right idea, Dallas. Maybe these yahoos wanted us to think they'd ridden off."

Dallas shrugged, although I thought he did it in a grudging manner, as though against his will. "Could be."

Without another word I pulled out the six-gun I was now carrying and began checking its load. Soon Hank, Pardee, and Clay Allison were doing the same with their weapons.

"Just what is it you've got in mind, Will?" Dallas finally asked.

In the distance I could see the roofs of the buildings that made up Twin Rifles. It was my town, the town I'd sworn to protect, the town I had to put my life on the line for when it came down to it. And this was one of those times. I holstered my six-gun before turning to my longtime friend. "It's like this, Dallas," I said in a serious tone of my own. "I can't remember any bandido ever running me out of the territory I rode through as a Texas Ranger."

"Hell, me neither!" I'd finally said some words that struck a chord in Dallas Bodeen's memory.

"Well, I ain't about to let no two-bit outlaw gang

keep me from coming back into my own town, especially when I'm the law in it," I said, a bit of a growl creeping into my voice.

"Now you've got the idea." I sensed that Dallas was getting almost as fired up as I was feeling. There was a sparkle of sorts in his eye, the kind I'd seen so long ago when he'd fight at the drop of a hat, back when we were both so young. Not another word needed to be spoken between us, for I knew that I could count on the man I was talking to.

It might have been a mile or so to the town limits, but I took that mile at an easy walk, hearing the horses of the rest of the group behind me as I rode nearer and nearer to Twin Rifles. I'll admit to being scared, for I never did care to be ambushed, but an old feeling was coming back to me now. The kind of feeling a lawman is supposed to have. The kind of feeling the people in town who hire him see in him. Being scared is one thing. But being scared of doing your job is another. Well, hoss, I might be scared but I wasn't afraid of walking into Twin Rifles and taking my chances with the Wells boys.

I didn't stop until I reached the city limits, my eyes carefully taking in the main street, looking for horses that I hadn't seen there before, men walking the streets who were just as out of place as their horses might be.

"This is where we part company, folks," I heard Clay Allison say off to my side.

"How's that?" I frowned at the youth.

"I'm needing something to cut the dust of this trail we been on, friend, so I think I'll head for the saloon," he said as though nothing else mattered. "Shoot, maybe I'll meet Chance or Wash and I can buy them a beer."

"Likely Chance more than Wash," I said, knowing my older boy had a liking for a daily beer if he had the money for it. "Let me ask you something, son," I said, as he was about to pull his reins and head for Ernie Johnson's saloon.

"Sure."

"Can I count on you if we do have a run-in with these Wells boys?" It was a question that didn't really need asking, for in my heart I knew good and well I'd be ferreting out Bob Wells and his gang of murderers. There was going to be some killing today, of that I was sure.

Young Allison had that crazy look about him now as he leaned across his saddle and said, "Like I told you, Marshal, as long as it's self-defense I don't care who I kill." Then, without another word, he swung his horse around and headed for the saloon at a nice easy walk.

I pulled out my fob and pocket watch and took a gander at the time. It was just after one o'clock in the afternoon. When I put the watch and fob back, I said to the others, "I'm heading for the Ferris House if any of you care to come along. Miss Margaret has likely fed most of her noon crowd, which will make it easier to get us some service."

"I'm all for that," Pardee said with an eager smile. I don't know whether it was being in the sun that had given him renewed strength or being invited to share a meal with us that gave him a new eagerness, but I was kind of glad to see it in the lad. If he was anything like Chance, he had a desire to fill his belly to overflowing after being on the trail for any length of time.

As for Catherine, she didn't say much of anything. The mention of Margaret Ferris's name had caught her attention, so I had a notion she would tag along to take a gander at the woman I said was mine more than to eat the food she might be serving.

"You tell your cook to put some food on the back burner ary you folks don't eat it all first," Hank said. "I've got to find me some equipment first off, and I think I see the store that's got it." He was staring off down the main street just past the bank. I wasn't sure what he was talking about, nor did he give me a chance to ask as he reined his horse to the right and followed the tracks out and around town, an action which at first seemed strange to me.

"Looks like it's the four of us," I said and proceeded to ride into town and pull up in front of the Ferris House. Catherine Innes made sure we could all see she was able to get off her horse all by herself. The one glimpse I got of her displayed a face that, though a mite battered, was still beautiful but at the same time had a tense look about it.

I was half expecting Margaret to come flying out through the front door to greet me, an action she'd done a time or two before when I'd returned from a long trip, but this time she must have been in the back, tending to her cooking. I could feel the tension build as I opened the door, not sure what to expect when Margaret Ferris and Catherine Innes caught sight of each other again.

"Margaret! Rachel!" I yelled once inside the door. It would take me a minute to adjust my eyes to the inside, having been on the trail all morning and putting up with the sun, but initially the place looked awful empty. "You back in the kitchen? You've got some customers."

Suddenly Margaret burst through the door from the kitchen, running straight for me. "Oh, Will!" she said as she embraced me in a tight hug. "You're all right, thank God," I thought I heard her whisper. The strange part of what she said was that I could hear her saying it through tears, and Margaret Ferris wasn't much of a crier.

It was when I looked toward the living area that I saw the reason for the woman in my arms crying like she was. Stepping out from behind a curtain was the bigger-than-life figure of Bob Wells, head of the Wells Gang.

And he had his six-gun trained right on Margaret Ferris and me.

CHAPTER

★ 27 ★

Another of Wells's henchmen had appeared out of nowhere by the time Pardee and Dallas entered the Ferris House. The gunman got the drop on both men before they could do anything. He motioned Pardee and Dallas away from the door and gathered up their weapons in the process. While he was at it, he took mine, too.

"I'm sorry, Will, but they said they'd kill Rachel if I didn't do what they told me," Margaret said, still sniffling. She seemed genuinely sorry for having drawn me into what I now knew to be a trap.

"Don't you worry, darlin'," I said, still holding her in my arms. I gave her a gentle pat on the back. Then, in a whisper, I added, "We'll get out of this somehow."

"I suppose this means we ain't gonna eat for a while," Pardee said with a straight face. I knew then he'd been listening to Chance too much and was trying to mimic my older boy's smart-alecky ways.

"I doubt you're gonna live long enough to eat, mister," Bob Wells said, a sneer on his face. He was acting like a confident son of a bitch. But then, that's usually how it is with a man once he's got a gun in his fist and figures he has the situation well in hand.

"Hey, boss." Another member of the Wells Gang said as he burst through the front door of the Ferris House. "They got Sam and Lou draped over a saddle out there!" Hank had handed Pardee the reins of the horse toting the dead men when he took off to get his equipment, whatever that was supposed to be. I remembered seeing Pardee tie the horse to the hitch rack out front as we reined in before Margaret's place.

"Now I *know* you folks ain't gonna live out the day," Bob Wells said, a bit of a growl added to his tone now. To the man who'd come in he said, "See, Charlie? I told you they didn't take off on us."

I gave Dallas no more than a short glance and saw he had his eye on me, as though silently saying "I told you so." I reckon he was right about the kind of men we were dealing with, a shifty no-good sort who'd likely kill their own mothers if they thought they could make a profit out of it. I found myself hating Bob Wells more and more as the day wore on. I think Dallas felt that hatred, too. And I *know* Margaret did. Listen, son, you don't take a woman's daughter hostage and threaten to kill the young lady without the mother feeling some kind of hate for you. Not on your life.

"What now?" I said to Bob Wells, knowing he likely

had bank robbery on his mind more than dealing with the lot of us.

"Back in there," he said, motioning us toward the kitchen Margaret had burst through only a minute or two ago. "Charlie, we got to get these birds out of sight and keep 'em there, understand?"

"Got you, boss," his henchman said and waved his gun, signaling for us to move into the kitchen of the Ferris House. When Wells and his cohort started to walk off, leaving Charlie all alone with the five of us, Charlie asked, "Where you going, boss?"

Over my shoulder I thought I saw a crooked sneer cross Bob Wells's face as he said, "The schedule's changed, Charlie. We ain't gonna wait for that damned bank to close. As soon as I can round up the rest of the boys, we'll rob it. As soon as you hear shooting, kill off every one of these intruders."

"You bet," Charlie said, apparently not troubled by the prospect of killing people in cold blood.

"You don't think you're gonna get away with this, do you?" I asked Wells before he had a chance to leave the Ferris House. Hell, I had to do something to stop this combination of robbery and murder, but all I could think of at the moment was asking a stupid question.

The gang leader stopped, holding the door half open as he turned to me and frowned. "Hell, yes, I'm gonna get away with it, Marshal. You people were downright unfriendly the last time me and my boys was here. This time I'm not only gonna take your money, I'll make you remember who the Wells Gang really is. But don't worry, Marshal, you won't be around to be concerned over it." Yes, the idea was I'd be dead as could be.

Then he was gone, and we all walked through the door to the kitchen. Rachel was sitting on the floor up against the far wall, her hands tied behind her back, her feet tied together, her mouth gagged. If Margaret was terrified for her daughter's safety, it was easy to see that the daughter felt the same way about her mother.

"Are you all right, honey?" Margaret said, rushing to her daughter's side. Rachel nodded, the fear still in her eyes as she took a grateful look at her mother, seeing that she, too, was all right. I do believe Margaret Ferris could have killed the gunman with her own hands right then and thought nothing of it. I couldn't blame her, either. I'd have done the same thing if it was my own boys.

For one split second I got to thinking then. Just where were my boys? I'd left Chance and Wash in charge of the town while I was gone. What had become of them? Had they tried something foolish when Wells and his gang rode into town and been silenced for their efforts? Or had Wells and his men made their way into Twin Rifles so silently that Chance and Wash didn't even know they were there? Could be. After all, I was sure that if any of these yahoos had openly ridden into town, why, they were still fresh enough in everyone's memory that there would have been shooting of some type by now. Maybe no one knew they were here . . . except the six of us.

"Don't bother taking that gag off'n her, lady," Charlie said. "You folks are all gonna look just like her in a few minutes."

"Good thing the kid ain't here," Dallas said with a

half grin. "I don't think he'd take to having any more of his rope cut to pieces."

I knew what he was talking about, remembering the night one of Wells's men had wandered into camp and had Dallas cut that rope of young Clay Allison's to pieces. Still, I didn't think it was too good a move to let this fellow know that there were more of us in town. Hell, it might just inspire the man to start his killing spree earlier than his boss had in mind, and I don't mind telling you I wasn't in any great hurry to meet my Maker.

"What's that? What did you say?" Charlie asked. I couldn't help but think that Dallas had gotten us into more trouble again. In fact, I thought I saw a half shameful look cross my old saddle pard's face just after he'd said his piece.

"Nothing," I said. "Nothing. Just an old riding pard we had oncet upon a time."

"Don't listen to 'em, mister," Pardee said with a disgruntled look. "They ain't nothing but a couple of old-timers spouting off. Been doing it all day. All day, can you believe it?" I reckon Pardee gave a convincing performance, for Charlie pretty much dismissed what Dallas had said from then on out.

I don't know where he came up with it, but Charlie had enough rope to hogtie a herd of calves, and he began making good use of it as he bound us up in the same manner he'd done to Rachel. He must have been good at it, too, for it didn't seem to take him very long. I don't think he'd figured out where he was going to get cloth to stuff our mouths with, for he had yet to do that.

"Oh, my God!" I suddenly heard Margaret say.

Something had apparently shocked her, but for the life of me I couldn't figure out what it was. All I could see was that she was staring at the clock. The time was going on two o'clock, which didn't mean a thing to me.

"What is it, Miss Margaret?" Pardee said in a voice of concern. "You got some food in the oven that's gonna burn, do you?" Apparently Pardee had also seen her glance at the clock, the same as I had. The trouble was he was sounding more and more like Chance, what with his concern for feeding his face and all.

"Listen, Mr. . . . . Charlie, is it?" Margaret said, although I thought I detected a mite of nervousness in her voice. "I have to get some wood from out back and build that fire up in the Dutch oven or that food is going to spoil. Can't you just untie me and let me go out back? I swear I won't try to get away. After all, you do have my daughter, and I'm not going to jeopardize her safety. You should know that."

But Charlie wasn't having any of it, not today anyway. "You move one inch, you old hag and I'll kill both you and her, do you understand?" he said, trying to sound tougher than need be.

Margaret looked as though she'd been slapped across the face, there was that much terror in her expression. Me, my eyes were about to fall out of my head. Not because of the ugly words this man was using on Margaret, you understand, but on account of what I saw filling the back door to the kitchen.

"That ain't too bright a thing to say," Chance said, but he wasn't worried about the outcome of making such a threat either, I don't think. Not one bit.

As soon as Charlie turned around, the first thing he saw was the long barrel of Chance's Colt Army Model .44 sticking right in his face, and that was a proposition you just didn't argue with. Not with my boy Chance. Not when he was sticking that long-barreled Colt of his in your face.

"Who are—" Charlie started to say.

"Put the goddamn six-shooter on the chopping block and shut up," Chance growled at the man, who did just that. But if he thought that was all he had to do to keep my older boy happy, he was sadly mistaken. As soon as the man had laid his six-gun down, Chance brought a piece of deadwood he'd been holding in his left hand up alongside Charlie's head. The thud it made on contact told everyone of us that the outlaw had been knocked out cold before he even began to fall to the floor.

"It sure is good to see you, son," I said, meaning every word of what I said. "Where you been?"

"Roll over on your sides, boys, and I'll cut you loose," Chance said, all but ignoring me and my question. To Margaret he said, "Found that big old piece of deadwood I told you about." With a wink and a smile, he added, "You just ask Pa. When it comes to eating a meal, I always get my chores done early."

I didn't know what in the hell he was talking about, and at the moment I didn't really care. "Cut me loose, boy" was all I could say. "They're fixing to open the ball, and we ain't been invited."

I was the second one Chance cut loose. The first one was Pardee, and you'd think the boy was rushing to meet the devil the way he grabbed up that pistol Charlie had laid on the chopping block and ran hell-for-leather out of the kitchen and out through the Ferris House. And I don't mind telling you that was awful fast for a man with busted-up bones carrying his body around.

"What do you want me to do?" Chance asked as he finished cutting my bonds. Not knowing the entire situation, at least he had the good sense to ask me what I wanted done.

"Keep an eye on this character and take care of the women," I said, rubbing my wrists to get the feel back in them. Chance never was one for being kept in the dark, so I said, "The damned Wells Gang is back in town and they ain't paying a social call, if you get my drift."

I tried to get up and run after the lad, but felt a couple of cracks in my knees as I got to my feet. I've had a mite of a hitch in my gitalong for some years now, so I knew I'd be more than a few feet behind Pardee as I made my way through the kitchen door and out past the community table. I was leaning over to pick up a six-gun out of the pile of firearms that had been thrown on the floor when I heard a woman's scream and a couple of shots. It sounded like it was coming from the bank!

Before I was out the door, I heard the distinctive voice of Pardee Taylor as he gave out a warning: *"They're robbing the bank!"*

The sun hit me full in the face as I pushed the front door open and charged onto the boardwalk out in front of the Ferris House. Pardee Taylor was there, too, but off to the left a few yards. And he'd been right in calling out his alarm to the people of Twin Rifles, for across the street and down maybe half a block was the Wells Gang, every last one of them either charging out of the bank with a satchel or two in hand or already out of the bank and trying to grab hold of a saddle and ride. But damn near every horse on the street was getting skittish about the gunfire that was going on now, making it hard for anyone to get mounted at all.

Pardee had already started trading shots with them, of that I was sure, for no sooner had I made myself visible on the street than I heard a couple of slugs thud into the house behind me. But not all of them missed their mark, for the next sound I heard was Pardee Taylor slamming into the front of the Ferris House. When I caught sight of him, he was sliding down the wall, his back against it, winding up in a sitting position, his six-gun still firmly in his grasp. The only thing different about him was that there was a blotch of dark red on his chest. It didn't put him out of commission, though. With both hands he took hold of that six-gun of his and shot one of the Wells Gang out of the saddle as the man attempted to cut and run, leaving town with one of the sacks of money from our bank. Dallas had been right: these birds worked fine in a flock, but as individuals they'd flee like scared rabbits. Thanks to Pardee at least one of them wouldn't make it out of town today. Not of his own free will, anyway.

I tossed a shot at another of the gang who had a sack of what I was sure was bank money and who had it in mind to get out of this shoot-out by running toward the opposite end of town. I missed him, but he never made it out of town, either. He started running down the boardwalk, away from the bank, which turned out to be the last mistake he ever made. It was then that Blacksnake Hank stepped out of Kelly's Hardware, directly in the path of this would-be bank robber. But he wasn't unarmed, for he had in hand the "equipment" he'd said he was looking for. Hank fired both barrels of a sawed-off shotgun into the belly of the man running at him, and the man fell lifeless to the ground.

"That'll teach you to kill *my* horses, you sorry ass," I heard Hank say in a relatively loud voice over the noise of the day. I reckon he wanted everyone to know what would happen to them if they harmed his animals. So much for two of these hombres.

"You can't do this to me, Bob Wells! You can't do this to me!" I heard Catherine Innes yell. Turning to the side I saw her standing there, a six-gun firmly grasped in both hands. As beautiful as she could be, this woman was a mite more than downright frustrated. She was killing mean! I saw her swing that revolver up and aim it at one of the men across the street as he was struggling to mount a horse. She fired but missed whoever she was aiming at—Bob Wells, I thought. All it did was make the horses that much more jittery. I don't know if it was Bob Wells who fired back at her or not, but whoever did hit her full in the chest, and she sank to the boardwalk unconscious, I thought.

Chance was standing at my side as soon as Catherine Innes went down, taking careful aim at what I could only assume was the man who had shot the woman I'd done a fair share of traveling with these past couple of weeks.

"Sorry son of a bitch," he growled when his aim proved true and another of the Wells Gang tumbled off a horse.

"What about Charlie, back there?" I asked, tossing a thumb over my shoulder at the Ferris House.

"I put another knot in his head," Chance said. "He ain't going no place except in his dreams." Then he added, "Besides, Dallas is watching him."

One of the last ones had managed to mount a horse, having picked up a sack of money a cohort of his had dropped when Pardee shot him out of the saddle a minute ago. He raced by us and likely would have made it out of town but for the mistake he made. You see, by the time all the shooting started, Clay Allison and Wash had wandered out of Ernie Johnson's saloon along with the rest of the patrons to see what was going on. This yahoo must have seen Wash go for his six-gun. My younger son was wearing a badge and likely realized that a bank robbery was in progress. The outlaw tossed a shot at Wash and hit him in the leg. Which was the mistake he made. Clay Allison had mentioned that he was on that cattle drive with Chance and Wash a while back, and I reckon he'd become good friends with my boys. At any rate, he didn't seem to take to seeing a friend get shot at. As soon as that outlaw's pistol went off, young Allison yanked that six-gun of his out and shot the rider out of his saddle before he could so much as get past Ernie Johnson's saloon. I knew he'd claim self-defense, but I also knew that no one in the town of Twin Rifles was going to press charges against Clay Allison for the shooting he did. As for the outlaw, well, I reckon he was dead, too. Lord knows, he sure wasn't doing an awful lot of moving once he hit the dust of the main street of Twin Rifles.

Then I heard someone let out a cry that set my blood to boiling again.

"Look! He's getting away! One of them's getting away!"

Somehow I knew it was Bob Wells.

I took a quick look about for a horse that wasn't too skittish to ride and saw that Pardee and Catherine weren't the only ones who'd been hit. At a glance I thought I counted three or four more of the people in Twin Rifles who had been shot by members of the Wells Gang. I reckon Bob Wells was serious about letting the people of our town know just who he and his gang were.

"Take my horse, Pa," Chance said, pointing to the hitching rail and one of the mustangs he had recently broken, a buckskin that looked a mite calmer than the rest of the horses in town. I was mounting up when I noticed that more than a handful of the men in Twin Rifles were doing the same thing.

"No! No!" I said, waving my hand for them not to do it. "Listen, you people, from what I can see, they ain't got our money. And that yahoo who just run out on us is my responsibility. I'll take care of him. You people just tend to fixing up the ones that've been shot."

"But, Will, *you've* been shot!" Hardy Beesum said in what sounded like an astonished tone of voice.

"That makes two of us, then, don't it?" I said, pointing out the stream of blood slowly but surely spreading down the man's arm. "Now, get these people doctored up like I told you." It wasn't a request, it was an order and he knew the difference.

"Will!" Dallas appeared in the doorway of the Ferris House. "Take this. You may need it," he said and tossed me his Henry rifle.

"Thanks, old hoss," I said. Leave it to Dallas. He could either get you in trouble or get you out of it. I reckon he was good at both. I was about to pull the reins of my horse when I saw Pardee Taylor still sitting up against the Ferris House wall. He looked even more bloodied than the last time I'd seen him sitting there, but I couldn't tell how bad the wound was, only that his chest was covered with blood. "Pardee!" I yelled.

"Yeah. Yeah, Will," I heard a weak voice say.

"Don't you go a-dying on me, boy. You saved the day, and by God, I'm proud of you." Just like Blacksnake Hank wanted everyone to know how he felt about his horses, I wanted everyone in earshot to know how I felt about Pardee Taylor. Mind you, that wasn't the way I'd planned to do it, but I didn't want to ride out after Bob Wells and come back later only to find out the boy had died on me. Everyone needs to be told they're doing a good job, especially when they're doing a good job.

"Don't worry about him, Pa. He's tougher than you think," Chance said, then proceeded to direct the people who were now out on the streets, trying to restore some sort of order in town.

I gave a quick glance in the direction of Catherine Innes and saw that Margaret and Rachel had knelt down beside her and were tending to her as best they could. The blood from her wound had spread, and her whole midsection was now crimson. I would have stopped to see how she was, but my instincts told me she was already dead, which wasn't going to help me catch up with Bob Wells.

So I lit out of town, bent on riding as fast as I could to catch up with the man I was sure was Bob Wells. Not that I was feeling like a spring chicken my own self. I'd only let out a few shots during that bank robbery and wasn't even sure I'd hit anyone. It seemed like damn little, once you thought of it, but sure did tire me some. I reckon it was when I glanced off to one side that I saw rather than felt the blood spreading down the side of my left arm. I must have been so caught up in trying to stop Wells and his henchmen that I didn't even notice the flesh wound I now had. That would also explain the sudden fatigue and thirst I was experiencing. But it didn't stop me. For a minute I thought I felt some of that light-headedness return to me, but it seemed to pass.

I kept right on going, easily picking up Bob Wells's trail outside of town. He was just as sloppy at leaving a trail as his gang had been on the whole, so I knew that he was fixing to have it out one way or another. The difference between us was that I didn't recall seeing this man get shot while the holdup was taking place in Twin Rifles.

Me, I wasn't worried about that. Oh, I'd been shot twice in as many weeks now and sure enough needed some time to heal, but as long as I had the ammunition I wasn't worried about whether or not Wells had been shot. We've got a saying in the Rangers, you see. Call it a credo if you like: "A man with right on his side cannot be stopped." Now, son, I know just as well as you do that a bullet will kill you dead as can be when it's put in the right place. I hadn't been a Texas Ranger for four or five years now, but there is something in that credo that keeps a man going, no matter how bad off he might be. So if Bob Wells had it in mind to kill me, and I truly believe he did, then let him have at it. The only thing I had on my mind was killing that goddamn murderer before he did the same to me.

He had headed north by west when he left town, riding hard over a stretch of barren land before coming on some rolling terrain that could be a surprise to anyone who wasn't careful about where he was going. Either I was getting old or this Bob Wells was thinking a mite faster than me. I was wondering what would happen if a body rode up on one of those washes and found himself right on top of the man he was chasing, when I did just that.

And there he was, Bob Wells, bigger than life. "Tut-tut, Marshal. You don't want to go reaching for that gun," he said with a sly grin that reminded me an awful lot of his cockiness back at the Ferris House. But he was the one who was holding the gun in his hand now. "You just drop that rifle and six-gun and get down off of that horse nice and easy and make your way on down here."

I did as he said, dropping my weapons and slowly climbing down from Chance's mustang, letting the reins drop to the ground. My mind was already trying to figure a way to get out of this scrape, but for the life of me I couldn't come up with one. The only thing that did come to mind was the fact that I still had that tinker's knife hanging around my neck. But as long as this Wells character had a gun trained on me, why, I'd likely die before I could put the blade in his sorry gullet. Somehow or other I had to distract him, get his attention on something else, something that would give me the split second I needed to throw that knife. Besides, I'd need every edge I could get with this man, for he didn't look as though he'd lost any of his health during that bank robbery. He wasn't bloodied at all, from what I could see of him.

"What now?" I asked, slowly making my way down the wash toward him. And as soon as the words were out I couldn't believe how stupid some of the questions I'd been asking today were.

"Why, you're gonna die, Marshal." For a second I thought he was getting too comfortable with what he intended to do to me, but any easiness he might have felt was quickly fading from the man. "You know, I took a look at Sam and Lou, the ones you brought into your town," he said as he approached me, his six-gun still in hand, still pointed straight at my brisket. "They were both knifed, as I recall. Sneaky things they are, those knives," he added, then slowly reached up over my shoulder and dug down the middle of my back, producing the tinker's knife from its sheath. "Fella tried using one of these things on me some years ago," he said, balancing the knife in his free hand.

"I suppose you did him in," I said.

"That's a fact. Killed him before he could throw it at me." You'd think he was proud as could be, the way he was boasting.

He was about to kill me. No doubt about that. A hundred thoughts raced through my mind then, most of them having to do with how in the hell I would get out of this fix. I had to do something and had to do it quick or I wouldn't be thinking anymore. But damn it, he had all my weapons!

It's amazing how fast you can think of things when you're boxed into a corner with no way out. You find ways of doing things that you would never have thought of under any other circumstances. With me it was weapons. All of a sudden it popped into my mind what I'd told my boys when they were youngsters and I was first teaching them to use rifles and handguns. I'd also made it a point to tell them that guns weren't the only weapons they could depend on in life. In fact, it's amazing what you've got left when someone takes away your rifle and six-gun. Take me, for example. Bob Wells had my rifle, six-gun, and knife. Me, I still had my fists. And this seemed about the right time to use them.

I reached up with my left hand and grabbed hold of his six-gun, pushing it aside as I hit him with a right cross that dazed him some. The revolver went off, the bullet ricocheting off the ground as he tried to yank the gun from my hand. My injured left arm wasn't strong enough, and he got his weapon back on the second yank as I hit him in the jaw again. Bob Wells was a fair-sized man, and he could take a punch with the best of them. He staggered back but had yet to hit the ground from any punch I'd thrown at him.

He was trying to do two things at once then. He was trying to get his balance again and trying to cock that six-gun and kill me, which seemed to be his main goal in life now. All I needed to see was that gun coming up and Bob Wells cocking it to know I was a dead man. I couldn't rush him, for he was too far back now and out of my range. Somehow I couldn't do anything but stand there. If death was coming my way, then so be it. I'd rather be shot in the front than shot between the shoulders running away from it. I'd taught my boys that, and this didn't seem to be the time to change my philosophy of life. Now, hoss, maybe that don't make a hell of a lot of sense to you, but it does to me. But then, you haven't been all of the places I have, either.

A shot rang out, and Bob Wells was the one it was aimed for. Before he could pull the trigger of his six-gun, he was reeling backward like some drunk. The gun went off as he brought it up, but the bullet went far astray from where I was standing. Then a second shot rang out, hitting him square in the chest, just like the first one had. He fell to the ground, dead.

In that one split second I knew I'd been given my life back, knew that my life had been spared. I looked up at Chance's mustang, where I'd dropped my six-gun and rifle.

"Well, I'll be damned," I murmured in a soft, unbelieving voice at what I saw.

"You're always telling me that most of us are damned, Will," my deputy said, a smile on his face. After I left town on the stagecoach I'd forgotten about Joshua. Forgotten about the wound he'd taken and whether or not he'd recover by the time I got back.

"You're looking mighty put out, Will. Mighty put out."

"You look just fine to me, Joshua. Just fine," I said, making my way up to where he stood.

"Why, they was right, you *have* been shot, Will," he said in pure amazement.

"Looks like I'll be needing a deputy right quick, don't it?" I said, finally developing a grateful smile of my own.

"So it would seem, Will. Look, you just pin that badge back on me when we get to town and let me take over," he said. "I'm getting to be fit as a fiddle anyway." He still had one arm in a sling, but I knew I could trust him with the town's best interests.

I suddenly felt very tired.

"You never lost the job, Joshua," I said with a smile.

"I know, Will. I know."

We packed the lifeless body of Bob Wells, the last of the Wells Gang, over his saddle. It took some doing, but between us we finally got it done.

Then we went home.

CHAPTER
★ 29 ★

Actually, Bob Wells wasn't the last of the Wells Gang. It was Charlie Spoaks, the man Chance had taken prisoner when the Twin Rifles bank was being robbed. He was the only one to survive the whole ordeal, and he turned out to be a real talker. From what Chance told me—and since there wasn't anyone in his gang alive enough to seek revenge on him—the man confessed to damn near every crime that had ever been committed, including the assassination of Lincoln. And I do believe Chance would have charged him with that, too, except that they already had the culprit who'd done that killing. By the time the law was through with Charlie Spoaks, I figured he'd spend a good deal of the rest of his life in prison. Either that or he'd wind up stretching some hemp when the judge was through with him. One thing was for sure, if he had to be tried anywhere outside of Twin Rifles for the rest of his crimes—and I knew good and well he likely would, if they didn't hang him first—I was going to let Chance or Wash escort the man to wherever that destination was. I'd had my fill of stagecoach riding for a while.

Pardee Taylor didn't die on me after all. Weak as I was feeling once Joshua and me got back to Twin Rifles, I still made my way to the doctor's office to find Pardee and a handful of others who'd been shot up, all being treated and all likely to survive their encounter with the Wells Gang.

"I'm right proud of you, son," I said, taking hold of Pardee's hand as I spoke to him. He'd lost consciousness and then regained it after the doctor took a slug out of his chest. "I meant what I said out there, too, about you saving the day, you know." I gave him a wink and a nod and added, "You know, ary I'm needing an extra deputy, why, I'll have Joshua here come look you up."

"Thanks, Will," Pardee said. From the smile on his face, I thought I knew that the lad had regained a whole bunch of his pride and confidence. Fact of the matter is, young Pardee Taylor had a whole new respect from the folks of Twin Rifles from that day on.

"Let me take a look at you, Marshal," Adam Riley, our town doctor, said. "That man needs some rest, and you need some tending to yourself."

Adam Riley was closer to Chance's age than mine, but he knew his profession so I didn't often argue with him. He eased off my shirt and began patching up the flesh wound in my arm. He was near through when Margaret came rushing through the door to his office.

"Oh, Will, are you all right?" she asked, at my side before the last of her words were out. "Joshua said you were up here getting tended to."

"He'll be fine, Margaret," Doc said with a confident smile. A tall young man, he had black hair and dark eyes that I sometimes thought to be mysterious in a way. And for a doctor he had a good muscular build about him. Come to think of it, I wouldn't have doubted that he could give Chance some competition if the two ever got to going at each other. "All I need to do is check that bandage on his head wound."

"I'll take care of it, Doc," Margaret said, suddenly horning in on the good doctor's profession. But that was to be expected, I supposed, for women did a lot more than cook and raise kids back then. They just never seemed to get the credit for all they did. I knew that Margaret Ferris had done her share of patch-up work, most of it long before Adam Riley came to our town and took up residence as a permanent doctor. "Why don't you check on your other patients?" she suggested, trying not to sound too pushy, I thought, although that was exactly what she was doing. "Or get some rest yourself, Doc. I daresay you've had a busy afternoon."

I reckon if anyone in Twin Rifles had patience, it was Doc Riley. He gave Margaret a smile and said, "I suppose I can leave this patient in your capable hands while I check on the others I've patched up today."

Margaret was gentle as could be in taking that wrapping off my head. At the medicine cabinet, she was picking out a bottle of salve as she said, "They must have been pretty close to you when they shot you."

"Huh?" I wasn't sure what she was talking about.

"That's quite a gunpowder burn you've got on your forehead."

"Gunpowder burn?" Now I was confused. I looked around the doctor's office until I spotted a small hand mirror, then looked into it to see what Margaret had been talking about. Sure enough, I hadn't just been grazed by a bullet, I also had a gunpowder burn, which at first struck me as kind of strange. Then I got to doing some thinking back to the day of that stagecoach attack by the Wells Gang. Margaret was nearly through applying a new bandage to my forehead by the time I'd gone over the whole thing.

"There, that should do for a while," she said with a smile.

"Tell me something, Margaret," I said, without even thinking of thanking the woman. I'll admit it was a thoughtless deed, but at the moment I was piecing things together, things that hadn't made sense before but suddenly became clear. "Catherine Innes, the woman who did the shooting out on the boardwalk—"

"She died about the same time you rode off after that man who escaped," she said, interrupting me.

"I see." Perhaps I'd never know for sure now. I walked over to the west window of Doc Riley's office and looked out at the sun, knowing it would be gone from the sky in a couple of hours.

I now had a pretty good idea of what had happened that day the Wells Gang attacked the stagecoach. I couldn't recall anyone opening the door and climbing in to the coach when the attack took place. And I'd assumed that a lucky shot had downed me, some of the luck being on my part, for that bullet could have struck me full in the head and killed me. But there was no way anyone could have shot me in the head and left gunpowder smudges like I'd just seen. That explained why Catherine had been so cautious when she tended to my bandage, always making sure that no one saw the wound but her. For anyone who saw the gunpowder on my forehead might get to thinking and come to the same conclusion I just did. They might realize that it was Catherine Innes, not one of the Wells Gang, who had shot me. But that wasn't quite correct, either, for Catherine Innes was indeed a member of the Wells Gang. She had to be if she'd shot me.

Pardee must have already been unconscious, kicked in the side by Bob Wells, for I was sure he would have mentioned something to me if he'd seen what happened. I never did ask Hank where he had picked up this woman. I made a mental note to do that later, knowing that he, too, was one of Doc Riley's patients today. He hadn't been shot like some of the rest of us, but he had an awful uncomfortable busted arm that had to be tended to right away.

"It was kind of strange, actually," Margaret said, joining me at the window.

"What's that?"

"The last thing she said was something about not being able to make a man love you. I wonder what she meant?" I could tell by the look in her eye and the mischievous raised eyebrow that Margaret Ferris definitely wanted to know what those words meant, likely figuring that if anyone knew it would be me.

I slowly put my arm around her waist and drew her near me, hoping I was doing it as softly and gently as I knew the woman would want me to. Then I looked her in the eye, hoping she'd know that I was telling the truth as I said, "It don't mean nothing, darlin'. It never did."

Someday maybe I'd tell Margaret Ferris about what went on during that stagecoach ride, including the deeds of the woman Catherine Innes. But that day was a long ways off. Right then I knew that I'd rather be aware of the woman at my side than think about a woman who almost killed me.

Margaret snuggled up close to me, working her own arm around my waist. I thought I saw a smile as I looked down at her and she said, "I'm glad you're home, Will. I missed you so."

I gave her a gentle squeeze with my one good arm. I was looking her square in the face when I said, "I missed you more than you'll ever know, darlin', more than you'll ever know."

When she returned the smile I knew that the words Margaret Ferris had spoken to me would always mean more to me than anything the woman known as Catherine Innes could ever have said to me.